Echoes of Unspoken

A Journey of Connection

by Moona Pirzadi

Endorsements

Dedication

To those who walk beside me on this journey of life and words, this book is as much yours as it is mine.

First and foremost, I want to express my deepest gratitude to the person who believed in this story before it even had a voice. Your unwavering support has been the quiet strength that carried me through every chapter. To my family and friends—your love, encouragement, and understanding allowed me the freedom to dream and create. You are the heart of everything I write.

To the readers who open these pages—you are the reason this story exists. Thank you for trusting these words to touch your lives. Your belief in the power of storytelling reminds me of the shared humanity that binds us all together. May this book offer you connection, hope, and a reminder that your own story is beautiful and worth telling.

To those who inspire me daily with their vulnerability and resilience—this book is dedicated to you. You are the unsung heroes of life's most profound moments. Your courage to share your truth has shown me the depth of what it means to be truly human.

And finally, to the quiet moments—the sunrises, the whispers of the wind, the laughter, and the tears—that shaped the soul of this book. It is in those fleeting moments that stories are born, and for them, I am forever grateful.

To Zaviyar, Mahbeer, & Zul Kifal—your light and laughter inspire every word I write. Thank you, little ones, for showing me the world through new eyes.

With all my heart, thank you.

About the Author

Maimoona Daved, known by her pen name Moona Pirzadi, is a 23-year-old debut author from Pakistan who believes in the transformative power of storytelling. Her writing isn't just words on a page—it's a journey into the chasms of human sentiment, exploring devotion, heartbreak, and the quiet strength that carries us through life's trials.

With a unique voice and a passion for raw, authentic stories, Moona draws readers into world, where vulnerability becomes courage and pain, transforms into beauty.

Through her stories, Moona hopes to inspire others to find hope in even the darkest moments and to see the extraordinary in the everyday.

Table of Contents

PART 1

PART 2

PART 3

*

PART 1

."In the quiet
between words,
love finds
its voice."

Prologue

Liana was seated on the carpet in her small book-covered flat, alternating between the noise of the outside world and refreshing silence. Light from the setting sun came through the window and, reaching the wooden floor, left stripes of golden light. One of the curtains flapped slightly as a light wind brought with it a faint essence of her favorite flower, jasmine. The people and activities outside were vibrant and in abundance, but here inside, her private space, and solace bubble as it is, time went slower, and she was able to pause for a moment. It was the most commonplace of the ordinary activities at the beginning of the day: getting home from the market, soaking in the silence within the four walls of her room, and lifting her pen to pour over the pages of her diary what the happenings of that day brought her.

But tonight, her reflections felt heavier, as though they carried the weight of something unsaid. Restless in a manner not quite described by words, it was as if her heart knew something she had yet to understand.

Her gaze fell upon the book that lay on the coffee table-a well-worn collection of Rumi's poetry, its spine cracked from years of opening and closing. She reached for it, her fingers tracing the rough edges of the pages, feeling the familiar comfort of the ancient text. She had read this book so many times that the words had become a part of her, coursing through her mind even when she was unaware of them. Yet tonight, something seemed to urge her to open the cover once more. She let the pages fall open at random, trusting that whatever she needed to read would find her.

Her eyes landed on the line: *"What you seek is seeking you."* The simplicity of the words hit her like never before. She had always been a seeker, one who felt there was more to life than what could be seen or touched. These were the years of search for something deeper, much above the routine of life, or the conversations one could share with friends like Daisy, Joseph, and Omer. They were her closest of friends, her confidants in so many ways, but even among them, part of her was always a bit remote, reaching toward something they could never seem to see.

She let out a low sigh now as she leaned back against the couch, her journal still open on her lap, open but untouched. The question swirled in her mind: What was she seeking? It was a question that had haunted her for as long as she could remember. At times, she felt it in the quiet moments between breaths, in the spaces between thoughts. Other times, it would tug on her like an invisible force, pulling her toward places and people she couldn't explain. And yet, all this seeking notwithstanding, she still hadn't found the answer.

But tonight, the words in the book felt personal, as though they were speaking directly to her soul. What if the thing she was seeking was also seeking her? The thought sent her heart racing, filled with an odd mix of hope and fear. She closed her eyes, allowing the thought to settle deep within her. Or perhaps this might be what it felt like to sense that all the deviation and questioning had a point. That the invisible thread she'd been pulling wasn't making her circle the same point but was instead guiding her toward something more correctly, someone with whom she had yet to cross paths.

She opened her eyes and stared at the ceiling, her mind racing. The world was so big, so filled with unknowns, yet in that moment, she felt that the answer was close to her grasp, just out of reach. Maybe she had never been ready to find it. Maybe it waited for her to stop searching, just to listen to the whisper of her own heart.

She reached for her pen and let her thoughts pour onto the pages of her journal:

"I feel like I've been searching for something my whole life, but I don't know what it is. Maybe it's not a place or a person, but a feeling of a sense of belonging, of being truly seen and understood. Perhaps the thing I'm seeking out is closer than I realize, tucked away within the quiet spaces between words, in the pauses of conversations. Maybe it's been there all along, waiting for me to notice."

She had stopped, tapping the pen against her lips, and went on: *"I've spent so much time looking for answers outside myself. But maybe that's what it is the truth is inside me. Maybe the journey isn't about finding something out there, it's about finding what's been in me all along."*

She closed the journal with the finality of setting the record straight, convincing herself that she had unraveled the knots in her mind and made sense of chaos through writing. Tonight, though, the answers stayed unreachable.

She got up from the floor and went to the window, opening it further to let the cool evening air wash over her. The twinkling city lights reminded her of the world that continued to move outside of her sanctuary. Yet, amidst all this vast, busy world, there was a stillness deep inside her, as if something lay in wait, waiting to be recognized by her and given room to grow.

Now, her thoughts moved to Omer, whose quiet presence had always been reassuring to her. They had been friends for many years now, having shared minutes upon minutes of laughter and silence, telling stories or confessions. But over the last year or so, she had sensed a shift between them, a tentative feeling that their connection was deepening-one neither of them spoke about, but both seemed to feel. It wasn't spoken, just as much in her life wasn't, hanging there in the middle of their conversations, waiting on a nod for development.

She had always admired Omer for his calm, his way of looking at the world in such a philosophically real way. He'd understand things without needing to explain them and accept mysteries in life without feeling the urge to solve them. She envied that about him, the ability just to be. Liana was always questioning, always seeking meaning in every interaction, every thought, every emotion.

What if she didn't need to search for them anymore? What if the answers lay inside her, waiting for her to stop running and listen?

She remembered Rumi's words again: "*What you seek is seeking you.*" The truth of those words sang in her so that she vibrated from the core of her very being. Maybe this was a time to cease this hard search. Maybe this was the time to trust the answers would come when she was ready to receive them.

As night started to fall and the city began to quieten, Liana closed the window and turned back to her journal, writing one last thought for the evening:

"I don't know what's waiting for me, but I can feel it. It's there, in the quiet moments, in the spaces between words. Whatever it is, I know it's seeking for me too."

With that, she snapped shut her journal and laid it on the bedstand beside her, lighter of heart, with a mind a little clearer. The path ahead was not clear, but for the first time in a long while, she felt ready to travel it. Whatever she was looking for, whatever was looking for her, she knew she'd find or it would find her. And in that silence, that unsaid understanding, she found her peace.

As days passed following the incident, Liana couldn't help but dwell upon the thought of the ties that existed with the people around her, the ties that were unformed and yet deep inside, and the tie within herself that she was longing for. She sat there in that bookstore and watched the faces pass by people with tales to be continued in pages they chose. Every book had an entire universe of emotions, ideas, and experiences, yet one thing that she could not get out of her head was that the stories she loved most were those echoing the heart's truths.

The bookstore had turned out to be her haven, placed in one quainter street lined with cafes and artisan shops, its cozy little space complete with towering shelves, cozy nooks, and comforting scents of aged paper and ink. It was here where stories came alive, and she reveled in the thought that each book held the potential to change someone's life as Rumi's poetry had transformed hers.

Every morning, she would unlock the heavy wooden door and inhale that now-familiar scent of paper and possibility. Daisy, her best friend and co-owner, would often turn up shortly afterward, filling the space with her laughter and warmth. It was a perfect combination because they could balance each other's quirks and eccentricity. While Liana was introspective, Daisy was effervescent-bubbling with energy and spontaneity. They put together an atmosphere where anyone would feel welcome.

Only, amidst this routine of restocking the shelves and making small talk with the regulars, Liana couldn't help but feel that something was left unsaid, tugging at her heart. Often, she would ask herself, dusting off the shelves and running her hands across spines of books that told many stories, *"What am I looking for? Love? Understanding? Freedom?"*

It was during one of these quieter times that their friend Joseph, who often came by, strolled into the store with a coffee in his hand and a mischievous smile on his face. *"Hey, you two! What's the word of the day?"* he called out, glancing between them.

Joseph could light up a room with his humor and charisma. He was that kind of friend who would make the mundane sound magical with a couple of well-placed jokes. Liana admired his easy ability with people; a trait she often envied. Daisy grinned, *"How about 'serendipity'? It's a good day for unexpected discoveries!"*

Joseph laughed and sipped his coffee. *"Serendipity, huh? Sounds like someone's trying to manifest something big!"* He cast Liana a knowing look that only served to make her heart race with an inexplicable mix of excitement and apprehension.

But the truth was that the idea of serendipity had by now become an attractive notion to Liana. What if the connections she was so desperate for were not a result of her pursuit, but the way the universe itself ordered and shaped her intersections with people and experiences that crossed her path? Perhaps it was all a sign, every interaction a hint from heaven, begging her to pause and take another look.

As they cleaned the shop throughout the afternoon, conversations flowed easily, and she found herself opening to him in ways in which she had not previously. First, she spoke of love and loss, the pang of unrealized longings, and her fascination with Rumi's verses that somehow gave a view to a world quite different from this one.

Joseph listened intently, his eyes alight with understanding. *"Love never is quite what one imagines it, Liana,"* he said. *"Sometimes it happens at the very moment when one least expects such happiness".*

The words had lingered in the air almost like an enduring melody, a soft reminder that sometimes life unfolded in mysterious ways. Liana could not help it if Joseph was right. Her heart was a compass pointing her in the right direction toward something-or someone-that would bring light into her life.

Days turned into weeks, and Liana started to observe her life from a different perspective. She listened more intently to the minutes: the sun showing shadowy figures on the pages of a book, the laughter of children playing in the park across the street, and the warmth of Omer's smile each time he visited the store. Each interaction felt charged with potential; every word held a message of something colossal.

One drizzly afternoon, while she sat by the window of the bookstore, watching droplets race down the glass, Liana felt a wave of introspection flood her. The world outside blurred, all colors in a tapestry of life, while her focus grew sharp. *"What am I afraid of?"* she mused to herself, confronted by unexplored parts of her psyche.

It was in that moment of solitude that the echo in her heart was undeniable. She yearned to be closer to Omer, a friend whose calm had always managed to ground her. They could talk about everything possible, yet something held her back from stepping across the threshold into lovers. What if he didn't feel this way? What if the friendship was too precious to risk?

Gazing out a rain-speckled window, her gaze trapped and shivering into the reflected image of herself, she decided to take a stand against them. She whispered to her captured soul, *"I can't live in the shadow of 'what ifs' anymore; it's time to open my arms to whatever this is-scary or otherwise."*.

In the evening, Liana found herself across from Omer at a small café not far from the bookstore. The air was thick with the smell of rich coffee and the sounds of soft jazz playing in the background. She felt the nervous excitement in her stomach as they settled into a cozy corner booth. Would this be the moment she finally opened up?

Omer leaned back in his chair, eyes contemplative as he watched her. *"You seem different tonight,"* he said, curiosity laced in his tone.

"I've been thinking a lot," Liana said, her heart beating in her chest. *"About us. About... everything.*

The weight of her words hung in the air between them, an almost palpable thing thick with possibility. She could see the flicker of understanding in Omer's eyes silent acknowledgment of the shift that had occurred in their relationship.

"What do you mean by 'everything'?" he asked, his tone low and inviting.

Liana took a deep breath as the candlelight danced warmly between them. *"I mean... I've realized I want more from life, more from our friendship. I don't know what that looks like yet, but I feel something deeper between us, something I cannot ignore."*

A smile burst across Omer's features, his face lighting up in such a way her heart skipped a beat. *"I've felt it too,"* he whispered. *"I just didn't know how to say it.*

Thick with unspoken words, the air crackled with tension; the tide changed in that middle space. Every word spoken, every held glance, every tantalizing smile-the bridge was being built across a thousand fathoms, joining hearts together. It was one of those conversations that had taken its good sweet time to happen, always there, just waiting for these two to reach out and touch.

That moment, the air itself was filled with unsaid sentences; the energy between them began to buck and heave like the waves of a changing tide. The words spoken, the turning of their eyes, the play of dimples in a smiling mouth-it was all like so many stones cast into the water, ripples joining ripples, spanning the gulf between hearts. This was more than a conversation overdue; this was a connection always there, waiting for two hearts to reach out and touch each other.

They talked for hours, deep into the well of feelings and fears, while the sounds of their laughter met with the strains of music floating from the café. Every secret shared, each confession given in vulnerability, was like losing those chains of doubt to freeing herself to exhilaration.

In the middle of the night, Liana felt something she had always yearned for, feeling that, in this connection with Omer, this wasn't just romance but a journey in self-discovery, with the getting of each other, and ultimately, love.

"I think we're onto something beautiful here," he said, laying his hand across the table to take hers.

In that simple gesture, Liana felt an echo of something immense promise of what was to come. It means that together they are stepping into a new realm of connection place where vulnerability meets courage and the unspoken is finding its voice.

"We'll figure it out together," she replied, her heart swelling with hope.

As they came out of the café, walking shoulder to shoulder in the dim light of streetlights, Liana felt the universe was conspiring for them. She was no longer in search of things; she started finding herself, finding Omer, and perhaps finding that connection deeper than ever.

The smile carved on her face as she walked back home that night, told of what was yet to come. It was a certainty that had eluded her for a long time, and just now, when this journey was about to start, she felt sure that what she was looking for love, connection, and understanding no longer out of reach; it was speaking to her from inside and urging her on to a future alive with possibility. The adventure ahead needed her to be prepared to explore the most hidden corners of her heart with Omer, Joseph, and Daisy by her side — whoever else it was that the universe kept in store for her.

She went to bed and reached for her journal once more. Now, the words seemed to flow from her pen with a fresh clarity:
"Tonight, I have learned that seeking is not a journey but a dance-the type of connection, linking us towards one another in ways we least expect. I am ready to dance, allowing the music to take me wherever it will. Whatever tomorrow brings, I know I will find my way, as long as what I seek is also seeking me."

And with those last words, she fell soundly asleep with her heart churning with the promise of tomorrow.

Chapter 1

When the Soul Spoke

"You are not a drop in the ocean. You are the entire ocean in a drop."
— Rumi

Liana woke up to the tender morning light creeping through her window and staining her bedroom with its golden-orange color. The world woke outside; the faraway chirping of birds mixed with the hum of traffic. She lay in bed for a moment, her mind drifting back to the conversation she had shared with Omer the night before. The connection they'd made felt like a fragile thread, binding their lives together in ways she hadn't foreseen.

The silence brought her back to the very moment when her voice was heard. "What do you want, Liana?"-she had asked herself during their talk one late night. It was fragile and echoed in her mind as something that had been asked to be out of her for years. Unspoken words hung heavily around, begging to be let free.

She sat up slowly, swung her legs over the side, and let the coolness of the floor around her. She went to the window and pulled back the curtains to let sunlight flood in and lighten up the room. She inhaled deeply, taking fresh morning air sweetly mingled with the fragrance of blooming jasmine wafting in from the outside. It reminded her of how, from chaos, something beautiful could be a metaphor for what was happening in her heart, which had become so anxious and yet so alive.

She showered quickly and then donned her favorite hippie-style dress: flowing, with minuscule patterns, the kind used by Persian carpets. As she looked in the mirror, she felt the surge of empowerment building up. Today is a day to know the unknown, to take a step into the uncertainty of my feelings. The thought coursed through her body, sending ripples of excitement mixed with trepidation.

She poured her cup of coffee, savoring the aroma, and went to her journal. She sat at the small, wooden table in her kitchen, flipping onto a fresh page. The lines just taunted her, screaming for her to pour out her thoughts. The pages were safe; they were a refuge that allowed her soul to speak unreservedly.

"What will today bring?" she started, the pen flowing with ease across the page. "I feel a shift inside of me, possibility blooming like the jasmine outside. Omer and I spoke last night, and it was different. It felt real. What does it mean for us?"

With every word, she felt the weight of her emotions coalesce into clarity. She wrote and wrote some more because that was her haven where her fears and desires could not judge her. She went on, "There's beauty in uncertainty, isn't there? Not knowing where the road will lead but being willing to take that first step regardless."

The memory of her talk with Omer came alive in her mind. They had sat under the stars-their laughter crescendoing into the night air as the talk deepened, and so did the mood in the atmosphere. "Liana," he had said, his voice barely above a whisper, "there's something about you that feels so... familiar. Like I've known you in another lifetime." The way he stared into her eyes then was as if he could see right through to her soul-a bond that went deeper than anything a friendship might offer.

After she had finished her entry, Liana checked the time and realized she needed to hustle to work. She grabbed her bag and ran out of the door, feeling a rush of excitement coursing through her veins as she speculated about what the day might bring. As she stepped onto the bustling street, the world outside greeted her with the familiar cacophony of life: car horns blaring, people chattering, and the faraway sounds of music. It was alive, much like her heart.

The bookstore was a few blocks away, situated between a used vintage shop and one of those coffee shops with delicious pastry. Each morning, its bright façade greeted her with the displays of newly arrived books and classic bestsellers. To enter meant to step into a world where her soul could run free.

As she entered, the soft chime of the doorbell announced her presence. Comforting scents of paper and ink embraced her warmly, and her shoulders unwound as she settled in. Daisy was already seated there, flipping through a pile of newly shipped books, her curls bouncing with each enthusiastic movement.

"Morning, sunshine!" Daisy called out, while her eyes sparkled. "You look radiant today! Did you dream about Omer or something?"

Giggling, Liana shook her head. "Not dreams, just too much thinking." She couldn't help it, but the color seemed to build up in her cheeks while mentioning Omer, her mind darting back to their recent conversations that indeed had managed to shift the very foundation of their relationship.

Daisy's grin broadened, her eyes shining with excitement. "Well, think! Tell me everything! Did you guys have a moment?"

Liana felt a leap in her chest at the enthusiasm in Daisy's voice. "We talked about... everything. I finally told him how I felt."

Daisy's eyes sparkled. "And? What did he say?"

"He felt the same way," Liana said, her tone barely above a whisper. "But now I'm terrified of what that means."
"Why? It's beautiful!" Daisy exclaimed, her excitement palpable. "You guys are perfect for each other! Just think of all the romantic moments to come! The late-night talks, the stolen glances, the poetry you could write together!"

Liana laughed, heartwarming by the thought. "I know, but what if it makes things complicated? What if we can't handle that change?"

Daisy leaned closer to her, wearing a somber expression for a moment. "Life is all about changes, Liana. That's the exciting part of it all. Besides, you can't let fear dictate your feelings. Just believe in what you both have.

She felt a huge surge of gratitude for her friend's consistent support. Daisy could always turn things around for her, where instead of fear, the beauty of uncertainty stared right into her eyes.

The morning flew by, getting ready for the day, shelving new arrivals, and arranging the store. The usual rhythm of customers in and out provided the background hum; Liana lost herself in the familiarity of the tasks at hand. Every time the doorbell jingled, her heart jumped with the hope it was Omer, knowing well that he would come later in the day.

As the hours passed, Liana interacted with the customers, pointing out books and tidbits about some of her favorite stories. A little girl in pigtails giggled as she reached for a bright pink picture book; an older man smiled and thanked her for suggesting a classic comfort novel during times gone bad. Each exchange reminded her of the depth of relationships in literature-a tapestry knitted from shared experiences, emotions, and insight.

As much as Liana enjoyed her day, she couldn't shake off that gnawing anxiety that had taken residence in the back of her mind. The question of what now seemed to hang heavy around her, weighing heavy upon her heart. The mere thought of crossing that invisible line from friendship into romance sent her running with her blood racing, both excited and fearful.
Joseph burst into the bookstore at noon, his boisterousness introducing a new wave of energy into the room. He strolled over to Liana, a mischievous glint in his eyes. "Well, if it isn't the lovebirds! How's the romantic tension brewing today?

The teasing jab had Liana's cheeks flushing in an instant, then Daisy couldn't help it; she burst out laughing. "You're just in time, Joseph. We were discussing the beauty of love and how Liana and Omer finally admitted their feelings for each other!"

Joseph's eyes widened to alarming widths. "Shut the front door! Are you serious? This is epic! You guys are going to be the cutest couple!"

Liana laughed self-consciously, the unwelcome concerns pushed to the back of her mind as they teased about the future. It was infectious, the playful energy of Joseph, and for that instant in time, all weight from her anxieties lifted to be replaced by lightness born from shared laughter.

But as the afternoon wore on and the sun hunched in its arc, streaking the evening sky in orange and purple shades, Liana had the feeling of that old, gnawing drag of anticipation. Omer was supposed to come after work, and every minute passing by made her heart run in what they might say, in what might change.

As evening fell, the bookstore took on warm, golden lights, invitingly appealing to the patrons who trickled in for last-minute purchases. She moved around the aisles, organizing and rearranging, all the while glancing at the door.

The door finally opened and Omer walked through it, the bell above softly chiming his entrance, the sun well below the horizon. He was casually dressed, his hair slightly tousled, an endearing quality that sent Liana's heart fluttering. Their eyes met over the room, a smile spreading across his face to light up his features.

"Hey, you!" he called, walking over to her.

Hi," she said, trying to sound steady.

"What have you been up to today? Is Daisy telling you how I've made her recommend poetry books all day?" He chuckled; his eyes were warm and inviting.

"She did," Liana replied, her heart thudding in her chest.
"And you? Are you ready to enter the world of Rumi with me?

Liana smiled, her heart racing with excitement. "Absolutely, his words always speak to me. It is as if he is talking to the very core of my being."

The corners of Omer's mouth turned up in pleasure as he took one step closer to her, electricity crackling in the air between them yet reassuring. "You know, I've been thinking about our conversation last night," he said, lowering his voice like they shared some sort of secret.

Liana's heart quickened. "Me too. I can't get it out of my head." Her emotions were racing, a surge of hope and fear and anticipation all contending for attention.

Omer took a deep breath as his face turned somber. "I know that stepping into this new phase may be daunting, but I seriously wish to.

Liana nodded, the weight of his words sinking in. "I want to, too, but I'm scared. What if we can't handle the change? What if it ends our friendship?"

Omer reached for her hand, and his touch sent waves of comforting warmth through her. "I believe our connection is strong enough to handle it. We've shared so much, Liana. I feel like we're meant to explore this together.

In that instant, she felt the threads of their lives weaving closer, binding them in a manner she had willed but could not quite understand. "Maybe it's time to take the leap of faith into what is yet to be," she said softly, her fears melting before the possibility.

They stood there, hand in hand, surrounded by the familiar comforts of the bookstore. Liana's heart swelled with hope, each beat resonating with the idea that perhaps their souls had always been speaking, waiting for the right moment to be heard.

"So," she said, a smile breaking across her face, "where do we start?"

How about we start with Rumi?" he suggested, the grin infectious. "We can read together, and we will go by his words."

Liana felt a spark of excitement go off in her chest. "I'd love that. A great way to begin this journey.

The way to the small reading nook in the corner of the bookstore was familiar, but Liana knew this was only the beginning. They were stepping into uncharted territory, entirely unaware of which path they might be traveling up, but filled with endless possibilities.

Together, they opened a collection of Rumi's poetry. As Omer started reading, his voice low and melodious, Liana felt the universe realign, each word vibrating with the rightness of what they shared between them. It was one of those transformative moments, an opening to delve into the depth of two feelings, and she was ready for it.

The soul had spoken, and in that sacred space, amidst the pages of poetry and the warmth of their friendship, Liana felt the stirrings of something profound—a love that was waiting to unfold.

Chapter 2

The Dance of Shadows

"When the soul lies down in that grass, the world is too full to talk about ideas, language, even the phrase each other doesn't make any sense." — Rumi

The days that followed unfolded like the petals of a flower in bloom, every moment peeling away to show new colors and layers in Liana's heart. Omer featured more richly and with more texture in her life as they hankered after the very careful dance between friendship and something deeper. Every glance they shared, every chuckle echoing through the bookstore, grew as a brushstroke on the developing canvas of their fledgling relationship.

She couldn't help but notice how every conversation was intimate in a way, arousing her excitement and at the same time, making her vulnerable. They plumbed the depths of poetry together-discussing Rumi and other poets whose verses spoke to their souls. Each session was a sanctuary in which their thoughts and emotions interwove into a tapestry of shared dreams and hopes.

One afternoon, as they settled into the nook at the back of the bookstore, Omer held a collection of Rumi's poems, his fingers brushing over the pages as if he were handling something sacred. *"This one always speaks to me,"* he said, reading aloud.

"The wound is the place where the Light enters you." His voice was steady and deep, reverberating in the quiet space around them.

As the words wrapped around her, Liana felt her heart swell. *"It's beautiful. It reminds me that the pain can provide a catalyst for growth."*

Omer looked at her, his eyes serious. *"Exactly. We have all been through something in life that serves to mold us. That is part of the reason, I think, that we connect on such a deep level. Both of us have felt lost yet are now finding one another".*

His words were so honest, that a chord resonated in her. *"You're right, it's like our scars brought us together somehow.*

The moments spent talking veered toward their pasts, toward the shadows that persisted below the surface. Liana spoke about her childhood, about how she had struggled to find her voice, about the journal that was her refuge. Omer spoke about his family, about expectations that were, at times, overpowering enough to suffocate him. With each word spoken, a layer of the soul shredded off; with each revelation, they moved closer.

One evening, closing the bookstore behind them, they found themselves walking in the nearby park where the setting sun was ablaze with orange and pink. The air was crisp, filled with the scent of fallen autumn leaves, and everything that lay in the sight of the golden hour was magical.

"It's amazing," Liana commented, pointing to the sky. *"It is like the universe is painting for us."*

Omer smiled, his eyes crinkling as a spark of mischief danced within them. *"Maybe it is. Perhaps we're the muses in some grand cosmic play."*

Liana laughed, a lightness washing over her. *"If that's the case, I hope we're not just supporting characters!"*

As they strolled down the path, their fingers eventually touched, and a spark flew across the space that lay between them. Her heart was racing in that thrilling mixture of fear and excitement;

the need to bridge the gap that seemed to hang between them was getting desperate.

"You see, I have believed this all along: that poetry is a kind of magic," Omer said after a while, breaking the silence. *"Healing and changing. Just like our conversations."*

Liana nodded, his words falling as weights upon her. *"It's so true. Every time we share our thoughts, it feels like we are weaving something beautiful together."*

Omer stopped walking and turned to her, his stare intense. *"You inspire me, Liana. You see the world with such depth. I feel like I'm discovering parts of myself that I didn't even know existed."*

Time froze as her breath got stuck in her throat, his voice echoing her feelings of vulnerability, and she could feel the silence speaking volumes of unspoken tension.

She, barely above a whisper, said, *"I feel the same way. You have awakened something in me that I thought was lost."*

Omer moved one step closer, their bodies almost touching. *"Maybe it is time we embrace this connection fully. No hesitations anymore-just. Us."*

Just as the words hovered in the air, a cold breeze whipped through the park and rustled the leaves above them. Liana shivered, though not so much because of the cold, but mixed feelings of excitement and fear. Was she ready to leap into the unknown?

At that moment, her mind was crossed by the shadow of complicated love. *"What if this complicates everything?"* Her voice had quavered a little. *"What if we can't bear the change?"*

Omer's face softened. *"All great love stories have their share of challenges, Liana. I'd rather take the risk than let fear hold us back. Life is too short to deny what we feel."*

Sincere words wrapped her like a warm hug; fires started to flare in her soul. She breathed in deeply, her resolve growing with it. *"You are right. I don't want some fear to rule my heart."*

It was as if he sensed her change, since Omer took her hand, interlocking their fingers. *"Then, together, let's see where this takes us."*

Liana smiled, her heart soaring. In that instant, the weight of the world lifted itself off her shoulders as the feeling of freedom and possibility took over. *"Together,"* she whispered in return, squeezing his hand soft and light.

They walked on, hand in hand, the world melting away as words were said of dreams and aspirations, hopes for the future, and fears that each had long carried. And with each word spoken,

Liana felt light, as though her burdensome past was slowly dissipating into the warmth of their connection.

Finally, they reached the edge of the park. Omer stopped, took in the view, and gasped. The city skyline was resplendent in a penumbra of twilight behind a dramatic backdrop to the emerging chapter of their lives. *"It's exquisite,"* he said, eyes sparkling.

"Like us," Liana added, the smile overspreading her face and refusing to be hidden.

Omer turned to her, his eyes serious with a genuine intensity that reached into her very soul. *"I think we are just beginning to discover the beauty within ourselves."*

With that, a couple strolled by, their laughter hanging in the air, and Liana felt longing ache within. She imagined the stolen moments they could share: the glances across the room, quiet conversations under star-filled skies, and the soft touch of hands clasped together in silent promise.

Still walking hand in hand, the weight of Liana's emotions, as much as their fingers bound, gravitated beyond the mere physical attraction to something deeper into their souls. But even as things warmed up between them, at the edges of her mind, shadows still lingered. Ghosts of past relationships, fears of vulnerability, and the haunting question if she could ever allow herself to love fully resurfaced, the whispered doubts echoing in her heart.

Omer must have felt the shift in her energy because he gently pulled her to a stop. *"Liana, what's going on in that head of yours?"* The words were a soothing balm against an inner turmoil brewing inside her chest.

She took a deep breath, panicked, and chose her words carefully. *"I want this... us. Still, at the same time, I am scared. What if we lose this beautiful friendship that we share?"*

He looked at her, his face unflinching. *"I promise to protect what we have. But you gotta believe in me, and most importantly, in yourself. Love can get messy, but simultaneously, it could be the most beautiful experience of our lives".*

Earnestness in his eyes ignited the spark of bravery within her. She so much wanted to be able to trust him, to take that leap of faith into the dark and this new era of her life.
"Okay," she whispered, determination shadowing in her voice. *"Let's take this leap together."*

Omer's face broke into a radiant smile, and in that instant, Liana knew they were sealing their relationship forever.

With every step they resumed, she felt lighter; the shadows of doubt dissipated in the warmth of their connection. First steps to a very beautiful journey, full of poetry and peals of laughter, discovering interwoven souls.

As night draped the city with its cloak, the hand-in-hand walk of Liana and Omer seemed to sway with the soft cacophony of laughter and chirping, or whatever slight sounds the world outside gave. In that sacred space amidst the beauty of twilight, she felt a sense of peace wash over her.

They were writing their love story word by word, and she was ready to see where it would take her.

Chapter 3

Whispers of Solitude

"Amid winter, I found there was, within me, an invincible summer."
— Albert Camus

And weeks turned into months, with Liana and Omer being drawn, every moment that passed, deeper into their connection the regions of love, friendship, and the convolutions within their souls. Their conversations were filled with enthusiasm about their new romance, yet beneath this excitement, tussles still went on with ghosts of their solitude threatening from time to time to creep back.

One brisk Saturday morning, Liana sat at her kitchen table with a steaming cup of tea snuggled between her hands. Soft morning light filtered through the window, casting gentle shadows to dance across the room. She opened her journal, full of thoughts, poetry, and bits and pieces of her daily life. This had become her refuge-a place where she could untangle her emotions and express those things which she did not say.

As she wrote, Liana felt the familiar pull of solitude. Despite the warmth of Omer's presence in her life, there were sometimes minutes when she longed for the quiet stillness of her own company. It was during these times that she could reflect, be in meditation, and connect with the deeper parts of her being.

"The wound is the place where the light enters you," she had read in Rumi's poems, and each time the words would come alive in her mind, they would seem to agree with what she had been through heartbreaks, healing. The joy that filled her heart through this relationship was almost in stark contrast to the scars of the past, and this in itself caused her to be in a state of dissonance more often than not.

She laid her pen down, staring out the window as her mind began to wander. The world outside was alive: children were playing in the park, couples strolled hand in hand, and the sound of laughter danced on the breeze. Yet amidst this vibrancy, she felt the quiet lingering feeling of solitude, a quiet reminder each person carried with them their stories, their wounds.

And in this, her mind wandered to Omer. He had become her friend, her confidant-the one who knew her on an intimate level that she did not expect. Their nights reading poetry furthered into discussions on life, philosophy, and the essence of love. Still, at quiet moments, stillness hailed in, where Liana did question if he, too, suffered under the weight of loneliness that sometimes draped over their shared moments of happiness.

That afternoon, she wanted to see a nearby art exhibition of local artists. The gallery was sandwiched between a busy café and vintage shops, something hidden from the usual gaze. As she went inside, she found the smell of paint and varnish in the air, with soft classical music playing in the background. Each spoke of stories, in muffled tones, of emotions and memories directly attached to the souls of the artists.

She made her way through the gallery, stopping in front of a huge canvas. The figure, solitary, was on the edge of a cliff, gazing out over a sea that was expansive under a stormy sky. Blues and grays tumbled heavily over the challenging hue of gold. It drew her to it, the raw emotion caught upon the canvas, resonating with her feelings of isolation and longing.

At that moment, she remembered the words of Omer: *"We find ourselves in the stillness, in the silence."* Indeed, it was true. Solitude might be a strong teacher, in times of reflection and growth. She wanted to share this experience with him, to invite him into her world of contemplation.

As she continued to explore the gallery, her phone buzzed in her pocket. It was a message from Omer: *"Hey! Are you free this evening? I found this new café that has amazing poetry readings."*

Liana's heart skipped a beat. *"Absolutely! I'll meet you there."*

The evening spent with him lits her spark within her. Maybe this was an opportunity to explore the ambiguities of their feelings more intensely together- shades of love and loneliness.

Later that evening, the setting sun saw Liana walking into the café. The string lights above the outdoor seating area cast a warm tangerine glow over the space; it was cozy, almost intimate. She finally found Omer on a tiny corner table with a book open in front of him, furrows lined on his forehead.

"Hey," she greeted, sliding into a seat across from him.

Omer looked up; his face broke into a smile that lit up his whole being. *"I'm so glad you made it. I've been looking forward to this all day."*

They ordered coffee and pastries. The conversation between them was easy. Liana felt the warmth of Omer's presence surround her, but she sensed in him, too, the underlying tension: comfort with each other, riddled by unspoken complexities hanging in the air.

As night began to fall, the cafe turned into a poetry-reading stage. Local poets took turns reciting their pieces of work; with every line, Liana's inspiration grew and grew. The words were flowing like water, strong yet vulnerable at the same time, intermingling in the capture of human experience.

The first poet spoke of love as a journey, showing how two souls navigate the serpentine paths of connection and loneliness. Liana listened with a heart full of recognition. *"Love is a dance between two souls, a rhythm that changes at each step,"* the poet said, but she found her gaze slipping sideways to catch Omer's eyes in the absolute understanding that silently bonded them.

As the night wore on, Liana's urge to share her thoughts took precedence. *"Solitude, I believe, is necessary for personal growth,"* she said aloud, her tone firm but meditative. "It allows us to confront our fears and insecurities, to understand ourselves on a deeper level.

Omer nodded, his eyes intent. *"I agree. But at times, that may also be a double-edged sword. It can bring clarity, yet when we do not find our balance, it will drive us to loneliness."*

Liana found his observation apt. *"It's finding that balance, isn't it? Being accepting of the solitude but seeking connection nonetheless."*

Their talk flowed without lags; both spoke about the puzzlement of life and the beauty of human association. Every cadence of thought seemed to walk deeper, beyond her into the space of vulnerability.

Later on, after the poetry reading was over, Omer said they could take a walk along the nearby river. The moon was hanging low in the sky, and that silvery glow across the water's surface was an ideal setting for their now budding connection.

The soft rustling of leaves and the sound of water lapping up gently against the shore replaced the sounds of the city as they walked. Liana breathed in the cool night air, feeling a peaceful sense wash over her.
"What is your favorite Rumi poem?" Omer asked, breaking the silence.

Liana smiled, and instantly, her mind began racing through the verses she loved most. *"It's hard to choose, but one that always resonates with me is, 'The only lasting beauty is the beauty of the heart.' Because it reminds me so that true beauty emanates from within."*

Omer stopped walking and turned back toward her. *"That's beautiful. And I think it's also a reminder that our points of connection with others are the things that enrich our souls. They reflect our inner beauty."*

The intensity of his eyes forced a stream of warmth to flow through her body. *"It's easy to lose sight of that sometimes, especially in a world that often places so much value on superficiality."*

He moved closer, his voice lowering. *"But we're not defined by the world around us; we create our narratives. Together".*

Standing face to face, Liana could feel her heart race with the energy between them alive. She wanted to bridge that distance and dissolve those barriers hanging in the air.

"Omer," she started; her voice shook just a little. "I want to follow this through, see where this connection goes. At the same time, though, I have to be upfront about my fears.

His face softened, and he took her hand, his fingers interlocking with hers. *"You can be honest with me. I'm here for it all joy, the uncertainty, the growth."*

At that moment, Liana knew their journey wasn't about romance but two souls intertwined, dancing through life, love, and all the shades in between.

"Then let's welcome it together," she said, her voice now steady.

Walking along the riverbank, with the moonlight guiding them into each other, Liana felt a deep sense of peace settle inside her. She was ready for the loneliness, the connection, the happiness, and the ambiguity. As long as Omer was by her side, she was ready to go through the labyrinth of their fledgling story, knowing every step would take them closer to the truth of what they were meant to be together.

Under the endless and unnumbered stars, Liana knew love was like a poetry of travels- beauty lay in shared moments, and magic lay in unsaid conversations. She breathed in deep, the cool night air, feeling the world lift off her shoulders, replaced by the promise of a new beginning.

Chapter 4

Echoes in the Silence

"You are not a drop in the ocean. You are the entire ocean in a drop."
— Rumi

When morning finally broke, Liana found herself sitting at her kitchen table, her journal again opened before her, the intimate details of her life: fears, hopes, and dreams that swirled within her like a tempest. She sipped her tea and let the early morning light streaming in through the window warm her thoughts and spread throughout her body. She had spent the whole evening wrapped in the brilliance of togetherness with Omer. His and her conversations were tapestries of insight and further vulnerabilities. But alone in her quiet home now, she reflected on the deeper implications of their relationship. She flipped the pages in her journal for comfort in the written word.

You are the entire ocean in a drop," she read aloud, savoring the greatness of the truths uttered by Rumi. It reminded her that within her lay such great depths of emotion and experience. Every individual they came across, and every experience they went through, was a layer added to their awareness of themselves and the world around them. Liana's mind turned to Omer, and she smiled at how his laughter seemed to ring right through the night air one night as they had taken a stroll by the river. The feel of his hand in hers, the look in his eyes-intense-made her heart flutter. But mixed with the joy, doubt followed. Was she ready to take up this journey?

Her reverie was cut short as the chime of her phone broke the silence, and she looked down to see a message from Omer: "*Good morning! Are you free for lunch today? I found a lovely little café by the river.*"

Liana's heart leaped. *"I'd love to!"* she replied with rapid fingers flying across the screen.
She got ready for the day, excited yet full of nerves. It was as if meeting Omer against this beautiful backdrop was an invitation to take this further between them.

Later, Liana came to this café, its outdoor seating area set under the trees in such an appealing way. The leaves seemed to filter the sun's rays through them, casting dappled patterns on the ground. Omer was already there, slouching back in his chair with a book open in front of him. He looked up as she approached, his face breaking into a warm smile that sent butterflies flying around in her stomach.

Hey there! It's awesome to see you here!" he said, standing to greet her with a gentle hug.

"I wouldn't miss it for the world," Liana replied-his presence was almost like home, she felt herself lighten up.

They sat at a small table; the murmur of the café and the gentle roar of the river became a background hum. As they perused the menu, Liana couldn't help but feel today was a chance to dig a little deeper.

When they had ordered food for themselves, Omer leaned forward, inquiring, his eyes sparkling with curiosity. *"What's been bothering you for some time now? I feel something different in your aura."*

Liana gathered her thoughts for a moment. *"I have been thinking about solitude and connection, how they interplay in our life. It is as though we need each one of them to grow, to be ourselves."*

Omer nodded an introspective expression on his face. *"That is indeed an interesting perspective. Solitude can be a teacher, but at the same time, it can also be isolating. It's all about finding the right balance."*

Amazingly, their conversation flowed so easily into the nooks and crannies of the human experience. Liana spoke of her solitude and how it had chiseled her haven in which she found herself. Omer, too, spoke of his loneliness-most of all, he said, during transition periods in life when the world outside became even vaguer.

"I've often felt that I'm moving alone in this world, even amid a crowd," he said. *"And then I met you, and everything moved. It was as though our souls all of a sudden knew each other."*

Liana felt a surge of warmth at the words. *"I feel it, too. We're like mirror images of one another, reflecting strengths and weaknesses alike."*

Their food arrived, and they took a moment to savor the flavors before them, but their conversation would not move from the depth of their connection. As they finished their plates, Omer pulled out the book he had read earlier and opened it to a marked page.
"I found this poem, and I feel that it captures what we have been talking about," he said, reading aloud:

The soul has ears to hear what the mind understands not. "

They seemed to hang suspended in the air between them, resonating deep within Liana. *"It's true,"* she mused. *"Our souls often know things before our minds catch up. I think that is why we are feeling drawn to each other so strongly. There is an unspoken understanding"*.

Omer smiled back, his eyes piercing. *"It's that kind of connection that transcends words. It's a dance of souls."*

It was then that a gentle breeze whispered in the leaves above them, and Liana closed her eyes, letting the moment wash over her. She almost felt that they were sheltered by a transparent bubble, cocooned from the chaos of the world around them. The laughter and chatter faded to the back, allowing only the soft hum of their mutual energy.

She spoke softly and in a hushed tone, *"You know, at times, I get scared, lose this bond we have built. I would never like it to slip through our fingers, like that exquisite dream."*

Omer leaned over across the table and laid his hand on top of hers. *"It will not fade if we nurture it. Love is a garden that needs attention, and tender loving care. Storms may rage, yet we have to continue tending it."*

His words were like a balm to her, keeping her feet on the ground. *"You're right. I want to be intentional about this, to explore what we can create together."*

Just at that moment, a couple walked by, laughing, caught up in that breathless moment of intimacy. Liana felt a pang of longing for the wholeness of love, the deep connection that seemed so effortlessly to flower between others. She glanced around at Omer, wondering if he felt the same.

"What do you see when you think about our future?" she asked, a tinge of vulnerability in her voice.

Omer was silent for a moment, lost in thought. *"I see a path taken together through laughter, trials, and growth. I see us discover new lands and share all our hopes and ambitions, standing together against all the buffets of life."*

Liana felt her heart swell with emotion at the vista he spoke about. *"That's nice. And what if we have obstacles? What if there are once more times of aloneness?"*

He didn't falter in his expression. *"Life is bumpy at times, and there may be tempests, but I believe these tempests serve to bind us together. We will brave the storms together."*

Emboldened by this, Liana grasped his hand firmly as her heartbeat increased. *"I want to embrace this journey with you. I'm ready to step into the unknown."*

Their eyes met, and in that deep of moments, the world disappeared. It was only them, two souls dancing in life.

Later on, as the sun gradually gave into an afternoon of lowering value, they set off for a walk along the riverbank. The water glittered in the light, much like their bond.

The time they spent walking, the burden of Liana's thoughts slowly began to dissipate. She had invested so much time being afraid of the unknown, worried about what lay ahead of her. With Omer, she felt a sense of peace, a security that love would survive through time and circumstance.

Suddenly, Omer stopped and pointed at the horizon. *"Look at that,"* he said, his eyes shining in a mixture of awe and wonder.

It was then that Liana saw a flock of birds flying in formation, their wings flickering brightly in the sun as they danced across the sky. *"They're so free,"* she whispered, as a tingle of inspiration washed over her.

"We can be like them," Omer said, his voice full of conviction. *"We can soar above our fears, let go into the freedom that comes with love and connection."*

Liana smiled, feeling the truth of his words echo within her. They continued, their steps buoyant, each one carrying them closer to the realization that their journey was just beginning.

They had strolled to a quiet area near the river when Omer suddenly faced her with an expression of true solemnity. *"Liana, I want you to know that I'm here for you. I want to explore not just the highs, but also the depths of who we are".*

His sincerity enveloped her like a warm embrace. *"Thank you, Omer; likewise. I want to unravel every layer, every shadow, and every light together."*

They sat in the grass, with the sun surrounding them in golden tones. Liana reclined backward, shut her eyes, and allowed the sounds of nature to take over.

"It is at moments like these that I remember all the things are so interrelated," she whispered. *"The river, the birds, us-we are all part of something much bigger."*

Omer nodded, but his eyes did not leave the water. *"That none of us ever stands alone. When we're alone, we are connected to the universe, to the other human beings in it."*

The depth of their conversation grew as layers of existence, through various philosophical threads and spiritual connections, bound them together. Liana felt the layers of her fears unraveling, replaced by an expansive sense of belonging. As the sun lowered itself to the horizon, casting its warmth across the landscape in shades of gold and orange, the conversation moved further from abstractions into more intimate reflective musings.

"Has this one moment ever happened that changed everything in your life?" Liana asked, turning to Omer, her heart pounding with the vulnerability of her question.

Omer's face slackened as he considered her words. *"Yes, I have. I was standing at a fork in the road in my lifetime when I felt utterly lost. I chanced upon a book of poetry, Rumi's work, and it felt like a lifeline. One particular poem spoke to my soul like it was written just for me."*

Liana's interest piqued, and she leaned forward. *"What did it say?"*

He paused a moment, then recited from memory, the words spilling from him like a song:

"The wound is the place where the Light enters you."

Liana felt the weight of his words settle between them. *"That's so profound. It speaks to the beauty of our pain and how it can lead us to enlightenment."*

Exactly," he said, his eyes mirroring shared understanding. *"I realized that my struggles didn't define me; they shaped me. It's how we respond to them that truly matters."*

Liana felt the emotion well up inside. *"It is comforting to know that our vulnerabilities can be strong. Often, I struggle with my open wounds and sometimes wonder if they will ever heal."*

Omer's touch was gentle as he reached for her hand; his anchoring grasp sent warmth into her skin. *"They will. Healing is a journey and not a destination. And to share that path with someone who understands- well, that makes all the difference."*

At this point, Liana was overwhelmed with emotions of gratitude for Omer. The connection they shared was fast becoming a haven, where their souls could take comfort and find strength.

With the sun already setting, dipping below the horizon into a blur of orange and purple hues, Liana remembered how beautiful it had sounded when they spoke of solitude earlier. She knew that to fulfill the richness of life, one needed both solitude and connection.

"Sometimes, I think solitude is necessary for personal growth," she said, her tone thoughtful. *"But it can be so lonely."*

"Loneliness can be a double-edged sword," Omer said. *"It teaches us to rely on ourselves, yet it makes us want connection even fiercer in its positivity."*

Liana nodded, appreciative of his insight. *"I want to learn how to embrace both. To be in peace with the solitude and share in joy at times of connection."*

Omer smiled. *"That's the journey we're on. Learning to dance between the two, allows each to inform the other."*

Then, with the oncoming of night, one million stars started twinkling in the wide-open sky above them. The world felt so big and limitless, as was the potential they carried within themselves.

"Look at the stars," Liana gazed, her eyes filled with wonder. *"Each one is like a dream waiting to be realized."*

Omer looked upwards, an appearance of depth on his face. *"And together, we can reach for those stars, making our dreams a reality. Yet sometimes, too, one has to remember that the journey is just as important as the destination."*

Liana felt a determination well up inside her. She wanted to embrace every moment, every experience they shared.

Suddenly, a cold breeze whirled through the clearing and sent a cold shiver down Liana's spine. She instinctively sidled closer to Omer, looking for warmth from him.

"Cold?" he asked, his features in an instant assuming a look of concern.

"A little," she replied barely in a whisper.
Omer wrapped his arm around her shoulder, tugging her into his side. *"Better?"*

Liana nodded, both comforted and electrified by the intimacy in the gesture. They sat this way for a moment in comfortingly silent repose, relishing the closeness, the quiet companionship that spoke volumes.

Then suddenly, Liana remembered something. *"You know, I've been writing about my dreams in my journal. Want to document this journey we're on."*

Omer turned to her, interested. *"What kinds of dreams?"*

Of all varieties, she bubbled over, but mostly dreams of love, of connection, of understanding. The experiences I record are those of laughter, of struggles, of the beauty of this unfolding journey.

"That sounds beautiful," he said, his eyes sparkling in admiration. *"May I read some of it?*

The thought caused a flutter of nervousness in Liana's chest, but she nodded. *"Of course. It's just an insider look into my thoughts, but I would love to share it with you."*

Omer squeezed her shoulder. *"I'd be honored. Your words have a way of touching the soul."*

Liana's face turned beet red as her whole body heated up. She wasn't the type to open her most inner thoughts to people, but with Omer, it felt right. It felt safe.

As they continued to watch the stars above them, Liana found herself considering how deep her feelings for Omer were. She felt just like a flower that began to open up, exposing the tender petals of her heart for the sun to touch and ensure their bonding.

As the night deepened and they began to take their leave, one from the other, something inside of Liana shifted: a piling sense that this was only the beginning of a beautiful chapter in her life.

"Whatever happens," she whispered as they walked side by side, *"I'm grateful for this moment. For you."*

Omer turned to her; his eyes, steady to hers: *"And I, for you, Liana. Let's continue to travel the echoes of our souls together.*

At that moment, Liana knew it-their bond meant so much more than just words or shared moments; it was a deep-seated travel of two souls across each other, finding meaning in the silence and strength in vulnerability.

As they stepped out into the night, holding hands, the future lay as an untravelled sea in front of them, full of possibilities and dreams to be accomplished.

We'll go through this together," Omer whispered his voice an almost healing balm against the trials of life.

And with the utterance of words, a bloom of hope took root within Liana's persuasion that no matter how dark things got out there, love would lead them through the echoes of silence into the light of communion.

Chapter 5

Whispers of Istanbul

"Travel brings power and love back into your life." — Rumi

The sun rose as a gold ribbon over her room and flooded its warmth inside. At the opened window, the smell of jasmine flowers filled her nose and revitalized her. A small flutter disturbed her chest because today heralded their long-awaited trip to Turkey.

She had always wanted to see the enchanting landscapes and the rich culture of this country, but doing it with Omer made all the difference. This was an opportunity for them to strengthen their bond and explore the world together. She was packing her suitcase, while her mind danced with excitement about what awaited her.

By the time she met Omer at the airport, her heart was racing with joy. There he was, his eyes shining with excitement, holding two tickets that glittered in the morning sun. *"Are you ready for adventure?"* he asked as his contagious smile set in.

"Yes!" Liana answered, feeling a run of excitement run down her body.

As they boarded the plane, Liana reflected on how this was going to allow them time to learn about not only the world but even the minute things in their relationship. They were leaving behind familiar grounds and stepping into the unknown together.

Finally, they landed in Istanbul, the city that straddled two continents, a city where East and West met in a breathtaking dance of culture and history. As they exited the airport, they felt the vibrant energy of the city grasp them, their senses ignited by the sounds, sights, and smells.

"Welcome to Istanbul!" Omer exclaimed, wide with wonder.

It was a quaint hotel room in Sultanahmet, and the balcony overlooked the magnificence of Hagia Sophia. Liana's heart swelled with excitement as she stared at the architectural genius.

"I just can't believe we're here," she said, still in awe of it.

"And that's only the beginning," Omer said, taking her hand.

Their first day was exhaustive owing to sightseeing. They haggled their way through the turmoil marking each corner of the Grand Bazaar maze of colors and aromas that seemed to throb with life. So Liana was enchanted by carpets with fancy patterns, glittering lanterns, and aromatic spices. She felt like a kid in a candy store, wide-eyed with wonder.

"Look at that!" she said, pointing to a stall filled with bright, colored Turkish ceramics.

They had meandered for hours among the stalls, tasted sweets, and jestingly haggled with the traders. She heard the sound of Omer's laughter, as much a keepsake she clung to as the trinkets they picked up together.

As they continued, Liana felt that connection not only to Omer but with the alive culture buzzing around them. *"I can see why you love this place,"* she said, her eyes bobbing with the frenzied atmosphere. *"It's alive with history."*

That evening, they found themselves at a charming rooftop restaurant with a view of the Bosphorus. The city twinkled below, highlighted by a myriad of lights. While they enjoyed traditional dishes, such as kebabs, mezes, and fresh baklava, Liana couldn't help but feel that the flavors of the food were matching the richness of their experience.

"It is magic," Omer said, raising his glass. *"To new adventures and unforgettable memories.*

"And to us," Liana completed, clinking her glass against his.

As the sun started to slowly dip below the horizon, painting the sky into hues of pink and purple, a feeling of peace settled within her. This was a lot more than just a trip; it was a journey of discovery of each other and most importantly of the world.

The next day, they took a tour of the famous Hagia Sophia as if they had entered into a different time in which nothing had yet happened. Its grandeur domes and overwhelmingly beautiful mosaics took their breath away. Liana wandered down a long hall with her fingertips, tracing the fine patterns on the walls as if she was touching history itself.

"It's incredible to think about all the souls who have walked through here," she said, her voice echoing softly off the stone.

Omer nodded. His face had turned thoughtful. *"It's a reminder that humanity is all connected. All of these stories, all of these lives, weaving together through time."*

They took turns reading Rumi's poems out loud, mingling verses with the echoes of the past. Liana was smitten by how Rumi's words seemed timeless, for this moment and place.

"The wound is the place where the Light enters you," Omer read, pausing after the words to let the weight of what he was reading sink in a bit. *"It's like he knew how much pain there is in the beauty of life."*

Liana's heart had resonated with a pang. *"His insight goes beyond time. It feels like he's guiding us on this journey."*

From there, they took to the streets of Istanbul, where the discovery of every nook and cranny came as a surprise: a small café buried deep in the alley, a local artist who painted broad landscapes, and street musicians playing and filling the atmosphere with vitality. They even found a small bookstore where Liana couldn't resist buying a collection of Rumi's poems, a tangible reminder of their trip.

And as the days dropped like a drag in Istanbul, they took a ferry across to the Asian side of the city. The wind ruffled their hair on deck as the skyline of Istanbul unfolded before them. Liana breathed in the salty sea air, feeling a rush of exhilaration.

"This is just like the scene of a dream," she said, eyes sparkling.

"And we're living it," Omer replied, looking afar.

After crossing over, the two strolled around the picturesque streets of Kadıköy, and there, they ran into the very vibrant market of all the fresh produce, flowers, and crafts that local people make with their hands. They had tasted fresh fruits and sweets, shared, laughed, and immersed in this joyous mood.

After some time, they came across a serene park where they could rest under the shade of trees standing since time immemorial. As they sat, Liana pulled out her journal and felt inspired to capture the beauty of this day.

"What are you writing?" Omer asked, leaning a bit into her.

"Just some thoughts about our journey," she returned, pen dancing across the page. *"It feels like each experience is a thread woven into the fabric of our lives."*

Omer watched her, his heart swelling with admiration. *"You have a way with words. I'd love to read more of your reflections."*

She smiled shyly. *"I'll share them with you. But you must promise to do the same."*

"Deal," he said, extending his pinky finger.

They locked their pinkies together, laughter bubbling between them, sealing the promise that their journey would be documented through their words and experiences.

In the evening, they went to the well-known Spice Bazaar: vibrant colors all over, and aromatic spices greeted them. The air was heavy with the scents of saffron, cinnamon, and dried fruits. Liana was in her element, and her senses were overwhelmed by these perfumed offerings.

"It's like a feast for the senses," she said, picking up a piece of dried apricot and offering it to Omer.

As they walked along the stalls, Liana suddenly came upon a small stall of intricately designed lanterns. Something about the glass with the warm glow captured her attention; she felt drawn to the colors.

"These are beautiful," she said, her fingers brushing against the cool glass.

Omer watched her, a smile playing on his lips. *"You light up like one of these lanterns when you see something you love."*
Liana felt her cheeks warm at his compliment. *"I just love how every piece tells a story."*

She picked a dainty lantern, whose color was the shades of the setting sun, and they went further into the bazaar, light-hearted.

As days turned into a week, Liana and Omer found themselves entwined, not just in experiences they had shared but in the moments of quiet understanding that needed no words. One evening, upon returning to their hotel, Liana saw Omer standing on their balcony, looking out into the city.

"What are you thinking about?" she asked softly, joining him.

He said, *"I was just thinking how the trip has changed me,"* looking out at the glitter of lights that are in Istanbul. *"It's as though I can feel the echoes of history, the whispers of those who came before us."*

Liana nodded, feeling a sort of connection with the city herself. *"It's as if we're part of a larger story, one that continues to unfold."*

Then and there, the realization dawned on Liana of how much this voyage had changed her. Closer to Omer she had become; it had also awakened the sense of wonder in the world. They were not only seeing new places but were discovering themselves and each other.

On the last day in Istanbul, they made a morning visit to the famous Blue Mosque, with its tall minarets featured against the sky. Coming inside the building, they were very amazed at just how big it felt. With every tile and stained glass window allowing filtered soft light to come in, the air was thick with awe and reverence.

She made her way toward and sat down in the quietest corner and shut her eyes, letting peace overcome her. Omer sat beside her, touching shoulders.

"This place feels sacred," he whispered.
Liana opened her eyes, her heart so emotional. *"It's a reminder of the beauty in faith and connection. It feels like a sanctuary."*

The two embraced the moment, letting stillness envelop them, for a few moments. Liana took out her journal, the tips of her fingers itching to write down her thoughts and feelings.

As Rumi said, '*The only lasting beauty is the beauty of the heart,*'" she mused, writing down the quote as she spoke. "*In places like this, I feel the truth of that. It's about what we carry inside us.*".

Omer nodded as a thoughtful expression crossed his face. "*I believe that. We can explore the world, but the real adventure is what we discover about ourselves along the way.*"

Liana smiled, feeling the sense of warmth and understanding blossom further between them. "It's been more than new sights on this journey; it's also been new insights into each other.

After a visit to the mosque, they wandered the streets of Istanbul one last time, seeing and listening with a bittersweet awareness that their journey was at its end.

"Let's take a moment to reflect on everything we've experienced," Omer said, guiding her toward a small café overlooking the Bosphorus.

With steaming cups of Turkish tea in their hands, they watched the boats glide across the water, its sun about to set. The sky became one huge canvas of tangerine, pinks, and purples, each oozing into another.

"What has been your favorite part of the trip?" Liana asked, her eyes bubbling with curiosity.

Omer leaned back into the couch, and an expression of contemplation faced the question. *"Honestly, it's hard to pick, but I think it's the moments we shared between sights: laughter, conversations, and the way we learned from each other."*

Liana felt the swell of affection in her heart as she listened. *"The same here. Every experience has stitched us closer together.*

As the sun was dipping below the horizon, Omer took out his phone and snapped a photo of the amazing view, then turned it on Liana. *"Say 'connection'!"*

Liana laughed, posing playfully. *"Connection!"* she retorted, enjoying the moment. Omer smiled and captured the image in his camera to remember this from their trip. *"This trip is just the beginning, Liana. There's so much more for us to explore together."*

Later that night, while packing bags in preparation for their departure, a surge of emotion overcame Liana. She wanted to put their experiences in her journal, wanting to preserve the memory of every moment with all the feelings.

She sat at the edge of her bed and began to write:

"Turkey has been a tapestry of experiences, each thread a moment sewn into my heart. Everything, from the whispers of Hagia Sophia to the bright colors of the Spice Bazaar, was printed in my soul. Omer turned no longer just my guide through the sights but a mirror to the intensity of my own heart. We have opened up to the beauty of togetherness, which interweaves our stories into the big plot of life."

She was writing and feeling the experiences come to rest in her heart deep appreciation for the journey they had undertaken together.

When Omer came into the room, he found her lost in thought, her pen dancing across the page. *"What are you writing about?"* he asked, his voice soft.

"Just reflecting on everything we've experienced," she replied, looking up at him. *"I want to remember every moment."*

Omer approached him, leaning against the wall as he watched her. *"You certainly have a gift with words. You capture life into words."*

Liana smiled, feeling shy under his gaze. *"Thank you. I believe this is an important record of our journey."*

"May I read it?" he asked, with a spark of interest in his eyes.

She hesitated but then nodded. *"Of course."*
She felt especially vulnerable sharing her journal with him, but he soothed her with an intent gaze. He read the words she had written aloud, and with every line spoken, it seemed they connected on a deeper level.
"Your words echo to me, Liana," he said after having finished. *"You look at the world from another angle."*

The beat of Liana's heart quickened. *"I just want to capture the beauty of this journey.*
Omer stepped closer, his face somber. *"You've done that and so much more. You've captured the beauty of us."*

Their eyes met, locked in a moment filled with unspoken understanding. Liana felt herself being pulled to him, a spark igniting deep within her at the warmth of his presence.

"I never want to lose this connection," she whispered, an edge of emotion high.

Omer leaned forward and tucked a strand of hair behind her ear. *"You won't. This is just the beginning, Liana. We'll carry this with us, no matter where life takes us."*

It was finally time for bed, having finished packing, and Liana couldn't believe how deep their connection reached. She now realized that the trip to Turkey wasn't about the travel at all; it was about the discovery of each other in ways she never thought possible.

Lying in bed, she felt her heart swell with thankfulness for the shared journey. It was almost as if the ripples of their experiences would go on, even after they got home.

"Tomorrow, we get back to our lives," she mused, *"but nothing will ever be the same."*

With this thought, she closed her eyes and dreamed of further adventures, ready to take whatever life had in store for them.

Chapter 6

Echoes of the Heart

"The wound is the place where the Light enters you." — Rumi

Omer's words made Liana's heart flutter. His gaze was steady, with a depth that seemed to reflect a regard she felt—perhaps for the first time in her life—was truly deserved. Unsaid feelings were jumping across from them, like a spark across space that separated them, an invisible thread drawing them closer.

Liana's voice softened as she mused, *"It's easy to forget that we are all part of something greater. But in these moments, I feel it so strongly-it's like the universe is reminding us to embrace every connection we make."*

Omer nodded slightly, his body leaning back and space between them, but not his eyes losing their depth as they held hers. *"Every encounter, every moment shared, paints another layer into our lives. I want to explore that with you sink deeper into these moments and see what direction they take us."*

His words felt so relatable to Liana. She had always envisioned life as this elaborate tapestry of moments thread representing a memory, something learned, or someone met. Weaving in a few more threads with Omer sounded exhilarating.

As the fire crackled, Liana couldn't help but reflect on their journey thus far. The trip to Istanbul had opened her eyes not just to the beauty of new places but also to the depths of her own heart. The way Omer urged her to share her thoughts, to dig deeper into her feelings, made her realize that she had held back parts of herself for too long.

She wanted to embrace the beauty of the vulnerability that came with true connection. With that thought, Liana placed her journal aside, feeling a shift within. *"Can I ask you something?"*

"Yes, of course," Omer said, his interest piqued.

"What is it that makes a connection profound you think shared experiences or something deeper?"

Omer mused on her question for a while. *"I think it is both. Times together create memories, but the depth comes from the understanding of souls. It is being vulnerable someone sees the parts of you that you do not show to everyone."*

Liana felt the warmth spread all over her body. *"I agree with you. I am just afraid to show this side of myself to let someone in completely."*

Omer's face softened. *"You don't have to be afraid of me, Liana. I want to know all of the light, the shadows, everything in between."*

As the fire kept on burning, the mood moved from cozy to intimate. Outside, the world faded down to nothing, like it didn't exist beyond their small cabin, which was being warmed by the tension growing between them.

"I think I have realized something," Liana whispered. *"Being with you, I feel alive. You wake up a part within me that was buried."* She had these words in her mind:

In the quiet chambers where feelings reside,
Echoes of heartbeats whisper inside.
Each pulse a story, each sigh a song,
A tapestry woven where souls can belong.
In laughter's embrace and in sorrow's deep swell,

The heart shares its secrets, its stories to tell.
Through trials and triumphs, in shadows and light,
Echoes of heart guide us through day and night.

Listen intently to the murmurs that call,
For within every echo, love conquers all.
In the dance of existence, in moments apart,
We find our reflections in echoes of heart.

Omer smiled tenderly as if he understood all too well. *"You are not alone in this feeling. Since Istanbul, since we started this journey together, I have felt a change. It is like we are all learning new things we thought never existed."*

Liana leaned into a leap of vulnerability, her heart racing. *"Can I tell you something no one's ever heard?"*

Omer nodded; his face was encouraging.

"I've been afraid to lose anyone. I've lost friends, I've lost family, and I can feel the mark on me from this. It makes me very wary of bringing others in, of loving fully." Her voice shook as she said this.

Omer leaned forward, his hand extended to take hers. *"You don't have to be afraid of me. We all carry our wounds, but they don't define us. They can guide us, teach us, and help us grow."*

Liana looked up into his eyes and saw there not just kindness but also an understanding of life's complexities. "*I want to believe that,*" she whispered.

"*You should. We face the darkness together, and then the light is beautiful,*" Omer said, his thumb gently stroking over her knuckles.

They sat in the soft glow of the fire, the shadows dancing on the walls. Suddenly, she felt a wave of safety. It was this moment of connection that was the essence of what she was seeking. Her fear of vulnerability slowly dissipated, replaced by an up-and-coming trust.

She said, "*Can we make a pact to explore this connection, to be open and honest with each other, no matter what?*"

Omer's smile broadened, and he squeezed her hand. "*Let's embrace this journey together, wherever it may lead.*"

Liana felt a wave of heat at his words feeling of fitting in that, until now, didn't exist. "*I'm ready,*" she whispered, feeling the weight of her fears lighten, if only just.

The next morning, they awoke to the warm light of dawn creeping in through the cabin windows. The world was covered with a layer of frost that shimmered in the soft light and was a true winter wonderland.

The hike in the early morning would turn the surroundings to be almost surreal with nature awakening in all its beauty. The crunch of the snow beneath their boots was the harmony, or rhythm, of their footsteps, echoing the unspoken bond that was growing between them.

They came upon a frozen lake, its surface shining like a sheet of glass in the pale sun. Omer was ever the adventurer and suggested they step out onto the ice. Liana did not feel comfortable with the suggestion; fears of slipping locked her mind.

"Trust me," Omer said, offering his hand. *"I won't let you fall."*

After a moment's hesitation, she took his hand and felt the sudden exhilaration mixed with fear as they stepped together onto the ice, cautiously at first, but soon breaking into laughter as solidity was discovered beneath their feet.

"This is amazing!" exclaimed Liana, whirling around with the cool air whizzing by.

Omer joined her, his laughter mingling with hers in a symphony of joy that echoed across the frozen lake. And in that instant, nothing else mattered: neither the past, nor the fears, nor the uncertainties. It was just the two of them, embracing the thrill of living.

As they returned to the cabin, clarity settled in for Liana. She was ready for whatever next came: her continuing journey of discovery and the flower of her new relationship with Omer.

They again sat around the fire that night, this time with mugs of spiced tea. Liana felt inspired to share yet another poem she'd been working on, inspired by their experiences.

"In the heart of winter, our souls intertwine,
Like branches of a tree, both yours and mine.
Through storms and stillness, we'll weather the night,
Together, we'll rise, our spirits ignited."

As she finished reading, her eyes rose to lock with Omer's, who was staring back at her in admiration.

"You have a gift, Liana," he said, his voice rich with sincerity. *"Your words capture the essence of what we're building together."*

"It's all because of you," she said, her voice low, a soft smile playing upon her lips. *"You have shown me beauty in vulnerability, in opening my heart."*

As the crackling of the fire and lengthening nighttime wore on, they shared stories, dreams, and laughter-one moment weaving another thread in the tapestry of their lives. Liana felt an exhilarating feeling of anticipation toward what lay ahead.

She felt that with every word spoken, with every glance they shared between them, this didn't feel like a climactic moment but an initiation toward something that, when the fire had already burnt out, was still echoing through their lives.

In the days that followed, Liana and Omer continued to see not just the beauty of nature but also the depths of their emotions. They found themselves telling each other more and more about their pasts, their fears, and their dreams, with every conversation drawing them closer and closer together.

They talked about Rumi; his words made them contemplate their journey. Many times, Liana found herself repeating the lines of the poems; it seemed to reverberate deep in her heart.

"Rumi once said, 'The only lasting beauty is the beauty of the heart,'" she revealed one evening, her voice firm. *"I believe that's true. What matters is how we connect with others and the love we share.*

Omer nodded thoughtfully. *"It's not just about the moments we create, but how they shape us. Each experience leaves an imprint on our hearts."*

As they packed up to head home, Liana was overcome with feelings of gratitude for the memories they had made and a sense of wonder about what the future may hold.

In the car on the way back, she reflected on the trip they had shared. It had been more than just one; it was a pivotal chapter in her life, a chapter that made her spirit rise again, and her heart opens up toward new horizons.

"What do you think is in store for us?" Liana asked, looking at Omer, who was driving.

"It's our thing, I think," he said, his voice introspective. *"We can decide to acknowledge it and see where it goes."*
Liana felt her heart flutter at the tenor of his words. *"I want to fully experience it. I don't want to hold back."*

Omer smiled and looked in her direction for an instant.

Chapter 7

New Horizons

*"Every new beginning comes from some other beginning's end." —
Seneca*

As the days turned into weeks, Liana and Omer fell back into their routines, the warmth of their mountain getaway still fresh in their hearts. But now, as spring materialized, so did a world awakening around them, promising new life.

One sunny Saturday afternoon, Liana decided she would go to some local art exhibition downtown. She had heard whispers of some sort of showcase featuring emerging artists, and such a notion of being surrounded by creativeness excited her. While walking down the vibrant streets, the air was filled with scents of blooming flowers and freshly brewed coffee.

The gallery was alive with energy, a kaleidoscope of colors and textures on the walls. Liana felt a surge of excitement as she stepped inside, her eyes immediately drawn to a large abstract painting that seemed to pulse with life. She stood mesmerized, letting the vivid brushstrokes wash over her.

"It's captivating, isn't it?" a voice interrupted her thoughts.

Turning, Liana found a tall woman with striking red hair and bright green eyes beside her. Confidence seemed to stay around her as comfortably as the air in this mountain pass, and Liana instantly felt an affinity.

"It is," Liana replied with a grin. *"There's something about it that speaks to me."*

Art does that, doesn't it?" she said with an expanding smile. *"I'm Clara, by the way, one of the artists represented here."*
"I'm Liana," she said, introducing herself. *"Your work is amazing! Which ones are yours?*

Clara motioned toward a series of smaller paintings that hung nearby. Teeming with life, each piece had swirling colors and abstract forms that somehow said something in their means.

"Those are mine," Clara said. *"I've been exploring the theme of connection and transformation. It's amazing how art captures emotions that sometimes we don't know how to tell."*

Liana felt an affinity with Clara the idea of changing resonated deep within her. *"I know what you mean, I've been on a path myself lately, learning to embrace change and openness of character."*

Clara's eyes sparkled with interest. *"That sounds interesting; I believe we're all in a constant state of evolution. What's inspired your journey?"*

As they strolled through the gallery, Liana spoke snippets about her story travels with Omer, the awakening she began to feel in Istanbul, and the deep connection they were forging. Clara listened intently, nodding in understanding.

"That's beautiful," Clara said when Liana was done. *"It sounds like you found someone who encourages your growth."*

Liana nodded, tucking a smile back into her lips. *"He does. Omer has been so supportive, pushing me to explore my creative side."*

"That is great; I think surrounding ourselves with the right people is important on our journey," Clara pondered. *"Speaking of which, I am having a get-together at my studio next week to celebrate the exhibition. That will be a good chance to meet other artists and creatives. You should come!"*

This invitation set Liana's heart racing. She was excited to be thrust into this new circle of people, yet at the same time, it brought a tinge of anxiety.

"I'd love to! I could use the inspiration," she replied, her voice steady."

A few days later, Liana came to Clara's studio. She felt excited and nervous. The studio was bright and airy, with half-finished canvases, splashes of paint, and an aroma of fresh coffee in the air. On every wall was a work of art from the initial sketches to almost finished; Clara's testimony to creativity.

She entered inside; the chatter of artists talking about their art and philosophies met her. She felt an energy surge in her as she listened to all that was said and began to appreciate such a place where creativity was renowned.

Clara spotted her and hurried over, a smile on her face. *"I'm so glad you made it! Come along. Let me introduce you to some of my friends."*

As Liana navigated her way through the crowd, she encountered a myriad of individuals, all carrying a story and a different creative field. There was Amir, the sculptor, who loved working with recycled materials; there was Selene, the photographer, capturing raw human emotions behind her camera lens.

Liana was energized by the conversations stirring around her, a breath of fresh air and an intricate outside of her world to at least consider other points of view.

In one instant, Clara brought them all together in a circle and asked them to talk about their journey through art. Liana listened, shown by stories full of resilience and passion.

Finally, it was her turn, and she harnessed her deepest breath in the warmth of the group in their support. *"I'm Liana, and recently, in my writing, I've found this power in vulnerability. I've been on a journey of self-discovery, and that has been beautiful."*

Nods of supportiveness filled the room; Liana felt a surge of encouragement. She spoke about her experiences with Omer, the time they spent together on adventures, and how art and connection opened her heart.

"Thank you for sharing, Liana," Selene said gently. *"Isn't it amazing? The way creativity connects us and processes feelings?"*

As the night wore on, Liana lost herself in conversations and laughter-a feeling she hadn't experienced in a very long while. She exchanged numbers with Clara, Amir, and Selene, all in hopes of staying in touch.

Later, circulating, Liana chanced upon Omer, who stood by the entrance, his eyes wide in a curious expression of admiration. He had come to support her, and at this, Liana's heart swelled with his presence.

"*Hey,*" she exclaimed, quickening her pace over to him. "I *did not expect to see you here!*"

"*I wanted to see this magic myself,*" he said, his face spreading into a grin. "*Clara mentioned to me that you would be here, and I could not resist.*"

Liana felt a warmth in her chest as she grinned at him. "*I have met the most fascinating people tonight. I cannot wait to introduce you.*"

Through the crowd, Liana introduced Omer to her new friends; he immediately relaxed into easy conversation with them. She watched, feeling a sense of gladness wash over her at the sight of him connecting with the people who had grown to be so important to her.

"*It amazes me how creativity bridges worlds,*" Omer said, his eyes shining with excitement as he listened to Amir describe his latest sculpture project.

Liana nodded in agreement. "*I feel like I'm stepping into a new chapter in my life. It's thrilling, along with a little bit overwhelming.*"

Omer leaned over to her and intertwined his fingers with hers. *"You're doing just great. Change is a wonderful journey to undertake, and I'm in this with you."*

By the time the night got to a close, Liana had found a level of closure she wasn't aware that she would have social bonding she had created, stories shared, and the support that was around her; all left her rejuvenated.

She walked back with Omer toward the car and thought that sometimes all one needs is a new beginning. "I'm so glad I came tonight," she said, turning to him. *"It feels like I'm discovering parts of myself I never knew existed."*

Omer smiled; his eyes softened. *"That's the beauty of life new connection opens a door to a different part of us. I'm proud of you for stepping out of your comfort zone."*

The words of Liana swelled her heart with warmth. She felt rejuvenated and more sure of herself toward whatever new horizons would befall her.

During the next weeks, Liana continued to nurture her friendship with Clara, Amir, and Selene. They were my sources of inspiration, a motivator who allowed me to go ahead and explore my creativity.

She found herself attending art workshops, collaborating on projects, and even co-hosting a poetry reading with Selene at a local café. With each experience, she felt deeper connections to her new friends and growth she had not imagined.

With the arrival of summer, as spring transitioned into the warmer season, Liana felt a surge of renewal coursing through her veins. The world seemed alive with possibility—and she was ready to embrace every moment.

Omer was a constant, continuing to support her in her pursuits while delving deeper into his passions. Weekends were spent hiking, capturing the beauty of nature behind the lens of a camera, and sharing dreams for the future.

One evening, as they were sitting on a hill overlooking the city, Liana turned to Omer with her heart full. "I have been thinking a lot about how far we have come along together. It is just like we are growing together, both of us pushing each other to explore new depths."

Omer nodded, looking out into the distance away from the horizon. *"It is a beautiful journey, isn't it? I think we're just getting started."*

Liana smiled, knowing in that instant the truth of his words. They were standing at the edge of something amazing, and she couldn't wait to see what other directions their paths would take them next.

Little did she know that as both of them went on to do their different creative journeys, a new set of challenges and experiences came along that would eventually question the bond they shared and force them to confront the very core of their being and what they wanted out of their lives.

As Liana and Omer walked back toward the car, she thought about those second chances. *"I am so glad I came tonight,"* she told him. *"Almost like I have found a new part of my soul I had never known."*

Omer the truth in the words touched a chord in his heart. They were standing on the threshold of something new, and wonderful, and she could hardly wait to see what fate had in store for them next.

One evening, coming back from an exhausting day of work, Omer called Liana into his apartment to show her some of the recent shots. *"I try to show emotions with my shots much like you with your poetry,"* he said, opening his digital gallery.

Liana leaned over his shoulder, her heart swelling with admiration. *"These are great, Omer! You have such a unique eye for detail. This one—"* she pointed to a photograph of a child laughing in the rain—*"is pure joy."*

Omer beamed with encouragement at her excitement. *"I am trying to create a project telling stories through my photographs. I have been thinking of exploring the themes of hope and resilience."*

Liana's heart went racing at the notion. *"That sounds amazing! You have such a talent for capturing the human experience. I would love to help in any manner that I could."*.

As the date of the exhibition drew near, anticipation reached a fever pitch. Clara and Liana worked on it with the other artists involved. Each brought her voice to the table in preparation. Liana poured her heart into her poems, filling them with all of the emotions she had felt on her journey.

The night of the exhibition found the gallery teeming with life. Liana stood beside Clara, bathed in technicolor artwork and hums of conversation. Viewers set their gaze upon the pieces, their responses mirroring what Liana and Clara hope to achieve in connection.

"This is amazing," Liana whispered, taking in the atmosphere. *"I can't believe we did this!"*

"You should be proud," Clara said, beaming. *"Your words are resonating with people. Just listen to their discussions."*

As Liana circulated amongst the guests, a sense of fulfillment washed over her. She shared her poetry, engaging in conversations that sparked inspiration and connection. Each reinforced her belief in the power of vulnerability and creativity.

Later that night, during one of the quiet moments that came in spurts while people celebrated around her, Liana saw Omer across the room, deep in conversation with Amir about photography. Her heart swelled at just the sight of him cast in the warm glow of the gallery lights.

She made her way over, a smile spreading across her face. *"Hey, you! How's the networking going?"*

Omer turned to him; his eyes sparkled with her presence. *"Great! Amir is sharing some fantastic insights on capturing the movement of photography."*

Liana felt a sense of pride for Omer, knowing he was embracing his passion. *"That's awesome; can't wait for the photos you will take after tonight."*

The moment the night drew to a close, Liana took to reflecting upon it. Indeed, the exhibition had been the turning point, illuminating new connections and fueling her further on the road of art. Yet, there was something deep inside of her that felt like something else was coming.

The next few days flew by in a haze of creativity and enthusiasm, but Liana couldn't rid herself of the feeling that she and Omer were standing on the edge of some great change. They had grown together so much, yet each was starting to find their way.

Summer was in full bloom, and so was the fascination of Liana for the new friendship and involvement in creative industries. She had spent her weekends writing with Clara, working on joint projects, and participating in the photography exhibitions of Selene. The stirrings of a deep, transformative journey seemed to grow more tangible the more time she spent with them.

One night, Clara invited Liana to her studio to celebrate their successful exhibition. The air was filled with artists mixing and mingling, sharing ideas and inspiration between sips of laughter and whiffs of the newly baked sweet aromas wafting through the air.

"Liana, you have to meet Leo!" exclaimed Clara, who, with an energetic presence, introduced a charismatic performance artist. *"He's been pushing the boundaries of creativity in ways so interesting.*

Thus, Liana had been struck by the love Leo had for performance art in using one's body to express emotions; this opened up new possibilities and creative expressions she had never tried before.

Over the coming weeks, Liana and Omer learned to balance their blossoming careers as artists with each other. As Liana began to take flight in her relationships with other artists, she couldn't avoid the perception that Omer was becoming increasingly brooding as he grappled with his artistic ambitions.

One evening, as they sat on the rooftop, looking out into the city, Liana turned to Omer with her heart heavy with her concern. *"I've noticed you've been quiet lately. Is everything okay?"*

Omer let out a deep sigh, his gaze far away. *"I'm just trying to figure out where I fit into all of this. I want to support your journey, but at the same time, I feel like I'm searching for my path."*

Liana reached for his hand, her heart aching for him. *"You're not alone in this, Omer. We're both exploring, and that's okay. I want us to grow together."* As weeks passed by, the weight of Liana's friendships and her relationship with Omer continued to shift and change. While she felt excited about the future, she also became aware of the sensitive balance needed between growth and connection. Days later, in Clara's studio, Liana was swept into a whirlwind of creativity, working with artists who stretched her limits. Amid the bedlam, she realized how such associations shaped her identity. At the same time, she had an overwhelming feeling that Omer needed her more than ever.

As they strolled home that evening, Liana was excitedly nervous. *"I want to share something with you, Omer,"* she started, her heart racing. *"I feel like we are at the cusp of something huge, both individually and together."*

Omer stopped and looked into her eyes intensely. *"I feel it too. It's exciting but also daunting. I just hope we can navigate it without losing each other."* Liana nodded, her voice full of resolution. *"We can. Let's make a promise: to communicate openly as we grow. I believe that no matter where life takes us, we can support each other."*

"I want that," Omer said, a hint of hope now fired in his eyes. *"Let's embrace this journey together.*

As they continued walking, Liana felt a new resolve on her art and the relationship. Both of them were undergoing some transformation, and together, they could navigate through the uncharted waters ahead. Little did they know that as summer wore on, new trials and experiences awaited them on excursions that tested their relationship and made them confront the very core of who they were and what they wanted from their lives.

Chapter 8

Threads of Destiny

"Love is not just found in the moments of joy; it's in the silent promises, the shared struggles, and the strength to stand together when the world pulls you apart."

When summer's heat wrapped the city, Liana wanted some time off from her maelstrom of arts and romantic thoughts. With all this life she had grown with Omer, Clara, and other artists, the buzz just became relentless. She wanted a moment of solitude, to reflect on her journey devoid of expectations of her relations.

As she sat in her favorite café one evening, sipping chamomile tea and journaling, Liana overheard snatches of conversation from the table next to her. Two women spoke rather excitedly, it seemed their upcoming arts-and-spirituality festival. Intrigued, she hunched over a little closer, curious about what they had planned.

"I heard it's going to be life-changing," added one woman, already with sparkles dancing in her eyes. *"Artists all over the world are going to come and share their work and experiences."*

The other woman joined in, *"I am not going to be able to stand waiting for the performances. That festival last year changed my life. It was so connected with the artwork and with people. It felt like discovering a part of myself that I never knew existed.*

An event like this would get Liana's heart racing at a mile a minute. Just thinking about new people, new experiences, and a place meant for creativity and spirituality, she could not resist. *"I need to be part of this,"* she whispered to herself, now determined this was it.

The other morning, Liana signed up for the festival. She was getting ready for it, excited and afraid at the same time. What if she didn't resonate with anyone? What if her art didn't click in such a crowd? These were thoughts that were running in her head while she prepared her bags for the journey ahead.

Chosen from a quiet, picturesque setting amidst rolling hills ringed by nature's beauty, the arrival introduced Liana to a myriad of artists, performers, and spiritual seekers alike, all filled with openness and creativity. The air was alive with anticipation and inspiration.

Walking around the grounds, Liana was impressed by the various forms of expression: installations created from recyclable materials, live performances combining dance and poetry, and workshops inviting participation in the study of creativity sans judgment. Every nook and corner of this festival seemed to celebrate life.

At one workshop, a woman by the name of Maya introduced herself. Maya was a performance artist working on themes related to identity and belonging. In a way, her expressive movements were speaking to Liana in a quest to find her place in this world. Afterward, they sat together, sharing stories of their journey.

Maya said, "*I left my corporate job to pursue art on a full-time basis, with eyes bright with the fire of passion. It was scary, yet I knew that I had to listen to my heart. With every performance, a part of my soul performs, and it grows with time as it keeps learning.*"

Liana related to how Maya did. "*I have walked a similar path,*" she shared. "*Writing poetry has become my refuge, yet at times, I feel lost amidst all the chaos that it creates within me.*"

Maya smiled wiser. *"Art can be both a refuge and a challenge. It forces us to confront our innermost fears and desires. Embrace the journey; it's all part of the process."*

As the festival rolled out, so did the myriad of workshops and performances that Liana joined in. Later, she joined a poetry slam where she had to share her work with other artists from walks of life different from hers. That was an exhilarating experience, and she felt the weight of her insecurities lift as the audience responded in encouragement and applause.

One afternoon, walking with her family and friends through the craft market at the festival, Liana found a stand that glittered in a riot of colored fabrics and also showcased an assortment of handmade jewelry. Standing behind the counter was a middle-aged woman, Amina, who exuded warmth and wisdom into the atmosphere. Liana picked up a delicate necklace made from colored beads, and Amina started talking.

Every piece I make tells a story, Amina said, her fingers moving quickly, placing the jewelry on her body. For me, art should speak to your soul. It roots us into our culture and each other.

Liana felt a tug at her heart. *"I am a poet,"* she said, feeling connected somehow to the artist. *"I write about connection and the journey of finding one's self."*

"Then you see," Amina said, her eyes shining. *"Art can reach over, create understanding where none existed before. We all travel a path, each of us in our way to gain connection."*

Amina's words thus inspired Liana to buy the necklace, feeling that it would remind her of promises to be kept to herself. This festival was a tapestry unfolding piece by piece, each incident weaving in a thread within the ever-changing narrative.

One evening, while the sun set behind the hills and the whole area of the festival turned to gold, Liana joined a group meditation sitting with the participation of a widely known spiritual teacher, Abdullah. As she sat down on the cushion in the circle of her fellow seekers, the atmosphere of quiet enveloped her.

"In the stillness, so we find ourselves," Abdullah began, his voice soft and melodious. *"Embrace the quiet, for it is there that the whispers of your soul can be heard."*

Liana closed her eyes and let go. She inhaled deeply, and all her cares lifted. Pictures swam in her mind: her life, her poetry, her love of Omer and Clara, and her new friends.

"The heart knows the way," Abdullah went on. *"Believe it. Follow your yearning, and you shall find your purpose."*
The depth of meditation washed clarity over Liana. It was not about finding her place in the world but every bend and turn along

the way home. Every person that she met at the festival added to her understanding of herself and her art.

The next morning, Liana woke up with a decision in her head: She would hold a small meeting for the artists she had brought together from the festival as an introductory space for sharing experiences and mutual support.

She drew this warm circle around herself, wherein Maya and Amina, among others, would share their stories and the art that shaped them. As they sat down, a sense of community began to build a tapestry of divergent voices sewn together by their love for creation and discovery.

"Let's share what inspires us," Liana said, heart racing with anticipation. *"We all have unique stories that can empower one another."*

Maya spoke about her transition from Corporate America as her "calling," while Amina spoke about finding her roots through her art. The conversations flowed freely, from personal experiences to philosophical contemplations.

"Art is a reflection of our souls," Maya said, emotion dripping from her voice. *"It allows us to tell that which words can't.".*

She listened closely as the ties of their stories began weaving a just reminder that bonds were in the making, every experience weaving into the insight about herself and everything in her surroundings.

The festival slowly came to an end, and Liana had much to be grateful for, taking in new experiences and meeting inspiring people who themselves sent her back in time to reconnect with the passion of her craft.

It was her last night, and she strolled onto the grounds alone to consider exactly what made her come here. Full and bright, the moon hung in the sky, shining down grey upon the landscape. She found a quiet spot and pulled out her journal to capture her thoughts.

She wrote, *"In every relationship, there is a fiber of me. With every touch, a stroke on the canvas of my soul, I learn to enjoy the uncertainty, which somehow is beautiful too."*

Writing, Liana realized that this experience at the festival became one of the significant chapters of her self-discovery path. She felt invigorated, ready to go back home and continue her life inspired with new insight.

The memories of the festival clung to her as she found her way home, each connection embroidered into her narrative. She had found enriching people and lessons in art, spirituality, and community that were beyond any price.

Back to her life with Omer, Clara, and friends, a sense of balance interwove a new appreciation of beauty in solitude and contact. Little did she know, her journey was very far from over. Instead, a whole new set of challenges was in store for her, ones that would test her perseverance and make her face the very core of her artistry and the relationships she had.

Chapter 9

Whispers of the Past

"Sometimes, the past whispers not to haunt us, but to remind us of the strength we've gathered from every broken piece we've learned to mend."

When autumn arrived, the strident colors of the festival finally did fade, leaving Liana with a sense of renewal regarding her purpose and longing for deeper contact. Far from those serene hills, to dive once again into the familiar world of chaotic energy the city breathed. And on to her journal, heart out day after day, recording events and lessons learned.

But as she fell back into the rhythm of life, an eerie nagging stepped right into her life. First, it had started with strange happenings: whispered conversations, as if listening in on her mind; fleeting glances of figures into her peripheral vision; and this inexplicable sense of being watched, as if the universe was trying to make some urgent communication pressed deep into her.

It was one of those evenings, spent at her favorite café, journaling, that she saw a book left unattended on a nearby table. The cover was frayed and titled *"Echoes of the Past."* A pull of curiosity urged her to pick it up. It was filled with poems and stories of love, loss, and the intertwining of souls across time. The words cut deep, stirring memories she had long buried.

"What is it about the past," she read, *"that clings to our present like a whisper on the wind? We carry our stories, light and dark, in the fabric of our being."*

Intrigued, Liana took the book home, promising herself that she would find its owner. That night, she opened it again, and the words seemed to leap off the page alive. Every poem seemed to speak to her very own heart, echoing her recent experiences and unspoken fears.

"You cannot run from your past," one read. *"It teaches you, leads you, and at times, it follows you.*

Liana shivered; somehow, she felt related even to the author himself, as though his experiences crossed paths with hers. This book turned out to be her inseparable companion, with every poem reflecting just her journey. Yet with every read page, she seemed to find some invisible thread pulling her closer and closer to this mystery of an author.

And for several days after that, Liana's world continued to unravel in unexpected ways. She started noting little coincidences: people she met, yet their stories seemed to share similarities with her own; events mirroring those of her past. There was always that little inquisitive antique shop she passed on evening walks that seemed to materialize overnight. A small, dark shop filled with a jumbled crowd of dusty relics, all seeming to cry out for someone to find and tell their stories.

One afternoon, curiosity finally got the better of her, and she ventured inside. Waves of aged wood and leather wafted thickly in the air as the soft tinkle of a bell in the shop announced her presence. The shopkeeper greeted her with a warmth-an elderly man with a sparkle in his eye.

Welcome, dear; what brings you into my little haven? He said in his voice full of warmth.

I'm not exactly sure, Liana answered as she peered around her at the treasures surrounding her. I've only been called here.

A dusty mirror-it ornate frame carved with intricate symbols entered her line of vision as she meandered through the shop. Standing closer, she felt herself entranced by its beauty. When she looked into the glass, for one fleeting second, she thought she saw another woman staring back at her, somebody familiar and yet not known.

That mirror has quite a history," he interrupted her thoughts. *"Once upon a time, it used to belong to a poet, a woman who had written her innermost feelings and dreams into a journal. She believed it could show one their true self."*
Liana's heart was already racing. *"Do you know what happened to her?*

Ah, she was lost long ago, but her words and the whispers of her spirit remained. And some would say her soul still walks this world, waiting for someone to find her story.

Compelled by an incomprehensible force, Liana bought the mirror, knowing it held a greater meaning. Later that night, she had it placed in her living room, and in that very instant, the space was different, breathed, and filled with potential and mystery.

Days turned into weeks and the resonances from the experiences of the festival mixed with the findings from her past. She was deep in her writing, penning poems based on the words of this mysterious author she had found in the café. The work thus began to assume a life of its own as if it were one with her thoughts and poems like conversations with the past.

One evening lost in thought, a name she read from the book sent her heart shivering: Isolde. The name was well-known; it belonged to her grandmother, who had grown up telling tales of love and loss intertwined with Liana's childhood. Could this book be related to the history of her family?

She wanted some answers and started going through the family tree, reading old letters and journals left by her grandmother. Every new find helped her compose another large puzzle of a woman who had loved so fiercely and then lost deeply.

"The heart remembers," it read in one of Isolde's old letters, *"even when the mind forgets. We carry the whispers of our ancestors within us."*

As this realization hit her, Liana felt the surge of knowledge that this wasn't just her journey but the continuance of the legacy left behind by her grandmother. The connection with her past was deepening, entwining more than ever before with her search for identity and belonging.

Tonight, as she opened her grandmother's journals, Liana came across this:

"In the heart of longing, a truth revealed itself to me,
My youth slowly came undone in echoing love,
A reflection of self, not in the face,
Rather a mirrored reflection in the echo of the soul for sacred space.

Those words set something aflame inside, a spark of recognition that managed to resound through the ages. It seemed Isolde was speaking directly to her across hundreds of years and prodded her to come closer to the truth about her lineage. Liana had an irrepressible longing to learn more about the poet to whom the mirror now belonged, perhaps whose essence still reverberated through the world.

She burst into his antique shop, with more questions and great expectations from the owner. But no sooner did she come in, indeed, the atmosphere changed: the shop now felt much heavier and darker. The shopkeeper was nowhere to be seen, and even the very shelves slid and folded, hiding corners where the relics of other worlds crowded each other.

The mirror she had bought suddenly hummed with life, drawing her into its power. She walked towards the mirror, beguiled by its call. As she peered into its depths, the surface of the mirror shimmered, and Liana gasped as images began to whirl inside its depth-visions of her grandmother, full of vigor and life, chanting verses in verse, with a fire of passion in her eyes.

"*Isolde!*" Liana breathed, mesmerized. The visions changed then, unfolding into a succession of events: times of joy, heartbreak, and an evil loss echoing through the ages. In one haunting vignette, she saw Isolde standing at the edge of a cliff, her eyes longing, filled with sorrow, clutching a journal tightly against her chest.

In that instant, Liana knew the depth of her journey through a mirror, a portal not only into her grandmother's past but toward those very innermost resources of herself; most intensely, she felt her connection with Isolde, finding therein a shared experience and struggles.

As the visions faded, Liana stumbled backward, out of breath and in shock. The revelations weighed upon her like an anchor, filling her with a cold mixture of dread and determination. She realized that she had to learn about the life of Isolde and what took her away, keeping all these secrets buried for such a very long time.

Upon returning home, Liana opened her journal, the weight of what that mirror had shown her lying heavy in her heart. She started writing down thoughts on paper, piece by piece:
"*In the echoes of the past, my purpose I find,*
In the shadows of loss, to the surface inclined.
With every word penned, the pain I do unearth,
To stories that still linger, like the rain.".

What had begun as something related to her artistry now evolved into a much deeper journey: one in which, to pay respect to her grandmother's life, she found echoes from pluralities that sculpted her very being.

As Liana finally fell into a fitful sleep that night, she dreamt of Isolde beckoning her toward some secret garden place where beauty and sorrow were intertwined. A thousand blooms are painted with vibrant colors, but the corners are filled with dancing shadows hinting at untold stories.

The voice whispered in the dream, "*Find the truth, Liana,*" Isolde's voice breathed. "*It is within the depths of your heart that you will find the whispers of our past. Embrace your journey, for it is not just your own.*"

She sat up abruptly and felt the heavy weight of the dream upon her. This was a call to find out the truth about her grandmother, reverberating within her, urging her toward some type of destiny. She knew further investigation was needed to find links that connected her with Isolde and maybe even brought out a deeper truth lost in time.

Determined to hunt down whatever still linked with Isolde the next morning, preparing to venture out again, Liana went on to research old newspaper cuttings or any records that might bring her clues about her grandmother's life in local archives and libraries.

The past was starting to collide with the present, and she felt that this journey ahead would, bit by bit, bring out not only the story of Isolde but also the truth of her own heart.

The weeks slowly took on the shape of days, but Liana's resolve sharpened with each passing minute. Every time that she visited the archives, another piece of life that Isolde led unraveled before her eyes, but the deeper she went, the more seriously entangled this web of family history got. She knew Isolde was not merely a poet, but a human who lived with passion deeply, love deeply, and loss deeply linked.

One afternoon, while rummaging through a stack of dust-soiled newspapers, Liana found one with which her heart leaped. Headline-blazed was the story *"Local Poetess Mysteriously Disappears: Family and Friends Left in Mourning."* Chronicled in detail was the life of Isolde and all her poetic fame, and the sudden chasm that her disappearance created.

"She was last seen at the cliffs," Liana said to herself, pondering the vision in the mirror. *"But why did she go there?"*

The article mentioned there had been a certain poem written shortly before Isolde vanished-one speaking of longing, and the inevitability of fate. The words danced across the page in a blur as Liana's shaking hands worked at copying them:

"When the heart speaks in silent tones,
And the soul wanders into unknown homes,
In the arms of darkness, I look for light,
For love that endures past the night."

These lines felt like a sort of key into Isolde's state of mind before she disappeared. Liana couldn't lose the feeling that in this story, something was missing, that there had been some hiding secret, some irregularity, that had pushed her grandmother over the edge.

She resolved to call Joseph, who had that knack for unearthing that one critical fact that would make all the difference. Across steaming mugs of coffee at their favorite café, she related her findings in that rising voice so characteristically upon the hare in flight.

"Joseph, you have to help me," she pleaded. *"Isolde's story isn't just about her; it is about me also. I feel that I am standing on the threshold of some great revelation which, like other big fish, may well be beyond my fathoming."*

Joseph leaned forward, interested. *"What do you think happened? Do you think that she left by her hand, or is it something more sinister?"*

"I'm not certain," Liana said, furrowing her brow, *"but I do know that she was in love with some figure unnamed in any of the articles or journals. There has to be a connection somewhere."*

"Let's dig deeper then," Joseph said. *"We can look for people who knew her, or even family members that could shed some light on her relationships.*

With Joseph, hope was afresh fired in Liana. Thus, both began jointly searching through historical records, interviewed some of their distant relatives, and even rummaged through social media in search of descendants of Isolde's friends. This then evolved into a hugely thrilling adventure wherein each lead promised more revelations of the past.

One afternoon brought them before an old woman named Miriam, a childhood friend of Isolde's, who is residing today in this very town. It was arranged to take place within a small flowered garden, each seemingly confirming the contentions of time. Liana and Joseph neared, and they could see Miriam tending to her plants, her face so weathered lit with a soft smile.

"You must be Liana," she said, her voice warm. *"Your grandmother spoke of you often, even in her silence. Come, sit with me."*
As they sat, Liana's heart was racing. It was finally going to connect with someone who had lived in Isolde's world.

"*What can you tell me about her?*" Liana asked, her voice barely above a whisper. "*What was she like?*"

Almost sparkling with reminiscences, Miriam spoke in a low, dreamy tone, "*She was a dreamer, just like you. Isolde could find the beauty in the mundane and turn the everyday moments of her life into exquisiteness in poetry. But then, she held a deeply sad sorrow.*"

"*Why did she disappear?*" Liana asked when curiosity got the better of her.

She was indecisive, her eyes wandering off to the sky. "*There were rumors of a love affair-somebody who had conquered her heart but wasn't destined to be. They say she often used to take to the cliffs to get away, to deliberate. It was some sort of refuge for her.*"

Liana felt the weight of Miriam's words settle in her chest. "*Did she ever talk of him?*

"*Only in her poems,*" Miriam said; her voice, though softer, didn't break. "*There was always a tinge of longing, a love that could never bloom to its full potential. She believed love was an edged sword-beautiful yet painful.*"

The revelation had hit Liana like a lightning bolt. "*Do you have any of her poems? Anything that may mention him?*"

Miriam nodded and fished a small, battered notebook from the bottom of her bag. *"These are the last verses she wrote before she vanished. I think you'll find them enlightening."*

As Liana held the notebook, she felt the surge of life running through her. Page after page was filled with Isolde's hand-thin, elongated letters, full of insight. She read on aloud:

"In shadows cast by fate's cruel hand,
Our love, a flame on shifting sand.
You were the wind, and I, the tree,
Bound together yet never free."

Liana's heart raced as her eyes read the lines, an undeniable connection to her grandmother's emotion. Every word was like something resonating from inside of her, something that lived through her, echoing in a timeless tunnel of love and loss.

"She was searching for something, wasn't she?" Liana whispered, barely audible.

Miriam nodded slowly. *"She sought closure, a way to reconcile her heart with the life she had chosen. But sometimes, in seeking, we lose ourselves."*

"Do you think she found what she was looking for?" asked Liana, shining-eyed.

Perhaps, mused Miriam, but the journey to finding oneself is never easy. It means going back to confront what was, and so often, the truths one finds out are more painful than the memories one clings to.

But it was as they were talking now that suddenly a tide of inspiration invaded Liana: her journey resembled Isolde's in deep ways, the call of understanding her grandmother's past, the bonding, and love intermingled with loss amidst complication of emotions.

"I think I need to go out to the cliffs," Liana said matter-of-factly. *"To honor Isolde, and maybe find a piece of myself along the way."*

Joseph listened intently, then nodded. "We should go together. There's something powerful about being in a place that holds so much history."

She smiled and let her eyes dance with understanding. *"The cliffs hold a lot of stories, my child. Just be ready for what you find."*

And then, when the sun was already lowering in the west and sent a golden glow across the garden, Liana felt that tranquility had washed over her. She was prepared to face what must be, not only because of Miriam's wisdom but also by Joseph's steadying presence.

The trip to the cliffs now turned into a pilgrimage to connect with Isolde, to honor her struggles, and to face the echoes that sculpted their lives. It was now that Liana realized how, across generations, a circle cut in a quest for love, meaning, and identity stitched their stories together in an undivided tapestry of shared experiences.

As she prepared for her travel that night, Liana wrote in her journal:

"In the quiet of the night, I hear the whispers of my past,
Each echo is a reminder love is never meant to last.
Yet in the shadows, I find the light,
Guiding me forward, into the night."

She closed the journal with hope in her heart and a spirit ready for what lay ahead, with her grandmother's legacy weighing heavily upon her heart. She was ready to take the next turn in her journey toward the cliffs awaiting her, carrying on their gentle hush the whispers of yesteryear.

So, wrapped under the cloak of stars, Liana prepared to seek the truth of Isolde's heart and her own, knowing full well that in the depth of love and loss lay the essence of life itself.

Chapter 10

The Tapestry of Lives

"Our lives are a tapestry, woven from threads of joy and sorrow, each stitch telling a story, each color adding depth—together, they create a masterpiece of resilience and love."

As Liana's journey took her toward the cliffs of her grandmother's past, a new character emerged across the sea, her story weaving a delicate thread into the tapestry of Liana's life. This was no accident—destiny, it seemed, had already begun stitching their paths together long before they met.

She stood at the edge of a vibrant bazaar, in one of Istanbul's busiest neighborhoods, where the aroma of spices and sweet pastries filled the air. Aylin, often described as a poet and an accomplished artist, sought refuge in her creations, painting her world with bright colors and intricate designs. But beneath this vibrant exterior lay a restless spirit, yearning for more than the routine and the carefully defined boundaries of existence.

"Life is but a canvas," Aylin would often say to her friends, *"and I am the brush. But what happens when the colors fade?"*

Her friends would nod, but no one truly understood the fire that burned inside her. They saw the joy in her art, the brightness of her soul, but Aylin carried a weight they could not see. The canvas of her life, once filled with light, had begun to lose its vibrancy.

Not always had Aylin's life been so optimistic. Growing up in a modest household, she had faced the pressures of family expectations. Her parents urged her to pursue medicine or engineering—fields that promised stability. Yet Aylin's heart pulsed with the rhythm of creativity, drawing her irresistibly toward the art that had always been her refuge.

One evening, Aylin attended an art exhibition in a gallery tucked away in one of the quieter corners of Istanbul. The gallery was lit with soft, warm light, and the pieces on display ranged from modern abstract sculptures to intricate traditional paintings. It was here that Aylin's life took an unplanned turn.

She found herself drawn to a particular sculpture, its shape so fluid yet profound. It depicted two figures intertwined in an eternal dance, their hands almost touching but never quite meeting. As she stared at the piece, contemplating its meaning, a voice broke her reverie.

"What do you see in this piece?"

Aylin turned to see a man standing beside her. He was tall, with an air of quiet confidence. His dark eyes sparkled with curiosity, as if he, too, was searching for something beyond the ordinary.

"I see a reflection of our fears and hopes," she replied softly, surprised by the depth of her own response. *"It's as if the artist captured the essence of our souls—forever reaching, but never quite connecting."*

He smiled, a slow, knowing smile. *"That's exactly what I was hoping to convey."*

Her breath caught. *"You're the artist?"*

"I am," he said, extending his hand. *"Emir."*

And so began the conversation that would change her life. What started as a casual discussion about art soon evolved into something deeper—a connection between two souls who recognized the same longing in each other. They spoke of hopes and dreams, of the struggle to balance passion and responsibility. Hours passed, unnoticed, as they wandered through the gallery, lost in their own world.

As their relationship blossomed, Aylin found herself torn between her love for Emir and the expectations of her family. Her parents had grown increasingly frustrated with her artistic pursuits, demanding she choose a more stable path.

"You're wasting your potential," her father scolded one evening, his voice heavy with disappointment. *"Art won't feed you, Aylin."*

That night, Aylin sat alone in her studio, staring at the blank canvas in front of her. The weight of her father's words pressed down on her, suffocating her creativity. She picked up her brush, but her hand trembled. What do I choose? she thought, her heart heavy with indecision. *The safe path or the one that sets my soul on fire?*

Emir sensed the turmoil within her. One evening, as they sat together by the Bosphorus, he took her hand and said softly, *"Art is not an option for you, Aylin. It's your voice. You have to follow it."*

But just when their love seemed to be at its strongest, fate intervened. Emir was offered the opportunity of a lifetime—to showcase his work at an art gallery in Paris. The catch? He would have to leave Istanbul for months.

"I cannot ask you to wait for me," he said, his voice thick with emotion. *"But I also cannot bear the thought of leaving you."*

Aylin's heart shattered into a thousand pieces, each one jagged and sharp. She wanted to be selfish, to beg him to stay. But how could she stand in the way of his dreams?

"Go," she whispered, tears spilling down her cheeks. *"You must follow your dreams."*

As Emir left, the world around Aylin dimmed. The vibrant colors of the bazaar, the warmth of the sun, even the beauty of her art— all of it faded without him. She tried to paint, but every canvas felt empty, every brushstroke hollow.

In her solitude, Aylin turned to the only other refuge she had known: poetry. Late at night, in the dim light of a small café, she scribbled her thoughts on the pages of her journal. One evening, she wrote:

"Love is a flame that warms the heart,
Yet distance can tear the world apart.
In shadows cast by time and space,
I search for solace in love's embrace."

Her words echoed through the café, catching the attention of a man sitting nearby. He was a poet himself, named Selim, and he was immediately captivated by the raw emotion in her verses.

"You have a gift," he said, approaching her after she finished. *"Why not share it with the world?"*

His words planted a seed of hope within her. Perhaps this was the nudge she needed to finally believe in herself as an artist, not just a painter, but a poet too. With Selim's encouragement, Aylin organized a poetry reading at the café, inviting local artists to share their work.

The night of the event, the café was filled with people eager to hear her words. As Aylin stood on stage, her hands trembled. But the moment she began to speak, her nerves melted away. The words flowed effortlessly, each line resonating with the audience.

"In every stroke of pain and joy,
I find the truth I can't destroy.
For art is the mirror of our soul,
Reflecting the pieces that make us whole."

The crowd erupted in applause, and for the first time in months, Aylin felt a sense of peace. She had found her voice again, and it was stronger than ever.

But even as her confidence grew, so did the ache of missing Emir. Their phone calls were bittersweet—filled with love, yet tainted by the distance between them.

One night, Emir's voice broke through the static, heavy with sadness. *"I miss you, Aylin. But I can't come back yet. I have to finish this project."*

Her heart clenched with the weight of longing. *"I understand,"* she whispered, though the words tasted like lies. *"But it's hard, being apart."*

Months passed, and just as Aylin began to find her footing as an artist, she received a phone call that shattered her world. Emir had been in an accident in Paris. He was in the hospital, unconscious.

The news hit her like a physical blow, knocking the breath from her lungs. Without hesitation, she booked a flight to Paris, her mind racing with fear and uncertainty.

When she arrived at the hospital, the sight of Emir lying so still, surrounded by machines, was almost too much to bear. She sat by his bedside, clutching his hand, tears streaming down her face. *"Please,"* she whispered, her voice cracking. *"Come back to me. You are my muse, my love. I need you to fight."*

Days turned into weeks as Aylin stayed by Emir's side, reading him her poetry, hoping that the words that had once brought them together would now bring him back to her.

"You are the colors in my world," she murmured one night, her voice barely audible over the hum of the machines. *"Without you, my canvas is blank."*

And then, one day, a miracle. Emir's eyes fluttered open. His voice was weak, but the words were clear.

"Aylin?"

Tears of relief spilled down her cheeks as she leaned over him. *"I'm here,"* she whispered, her heart bursting with joy. *"You're going to be okay."*

In that moment, Aylin realized something profound: love wasn't just about passion and connection. It was about resilience, sacrifice, and standing by each other through the darkest of times. Their journey had been filled with obstacles, but it was those very challenges that had forged their bond into something unbreakable.

When they finally returned to Istanbul, Aylin felt as if she had been reborn. The colors of her world were vibrant once again, but this time, they were painted with the hues of shared experiences and hard-won victories.

She stood beside Emir, their hands intertwined, ready to face whatever the future held—together, the warm Istanbul breeze weaving through their hair, *Aylin's voice softened,*

"Emir, do you believe in fate? That our souls were meant to meet, to collide in this strange dance of love and longing?"

Emir smiled gently, his eyes meeting hers with a depth that only love forged in trials could hold.

"Perhaps, my love, it is not fate that binds us but the choices we make, the sacrifices that shape our hearts. We were always the artists of our own story."

Aylin nodded, her fingers tracing the faint lines of his palm. She could feel the weight of those words, the years of longing, separation, and eventual reunion converging into this one moment.

"Then let us paint a new story together," she whispered. *"One where the colors never fade, where love becomes the ink that writes the rest of our lives."*

And in that moment, beneath the golden Turkish sun, they knew — life was not a fixed path, but an endless canvas, and together, they would fill it with the hues of love, resilience, and endless possibility.

As Aylin rested her head on Emir's shoulder, the rhythmic pulse of his heartbeat was a steady reminder of the life they had almost lost. They stood in silence, the city of Istanbul alive around them, yet they existed in a world of their own—suspended between past heartache and a future unwritten.

"Do you remember the first time we spoke about art?" Aylin asked softly, her voice carrying a note of nostalgia. *"You told me that every piece of art is a reflection of the soul, and I never forgot that."*

"I remember," Emir replied, his voice laced with fondness. *"You said art is the language of love, and I knew then that you understood more than just technique—you understood the depth of feeling behind every stroke."*

Aylin smiled, the memory filling her with warmth. But beneath the surface, there was a quiet reflection—of everything they had endured to stand here together. Life had tested them in ways neither could have predicted, yet here they were, still intertwined like threads in a grand tapestry.

"I'm scared sometimes," she confessed after a pause, her fingers tightening around his. *"Of losing what we have. Of time stealing away the colors we've painted."*

"Then we must keep painting," Emir whispered, turning to face her fully. *"Not because we fear the canvas will fade, but because every day, every moment, is an opportunity to add more. Love doesn't stay the same—it grows, it shifts, just like the brushstrokes on a painting."*

Tears welled up in Aylin's eyes, but they weren't from sadness. They were from the overwhelming beauty of this truth—the understanding that love, like art, was never static. It was ever-changing, ever-growing, shaped by every experience, every hardship, and every joy.

"Let's not paint in fear," she said, her voice trembling slightly. *"Let's paint in hope."*

As the sun began to set, casting a golden hue across the Bosphorus, Aylin reached into her bag and pulled out a notebook, one she had carried with her for years. Its pages were filled with sketches, poems, and thoughts—snippets of her journey, each word a reflection of her heart.

She opened it to a page where she had scribbled a quote she'd once read in one of Rumi's collections. She traced her fingers over the ink and read aloud:

"You are not a drop in the ocean. You are the entire ocean, in a drop."

Emir smiled at the words, familiar and comforting, and leaned closer. *"That's how I've always seen you, Aylin. You carry the whole world inside you—the joy, the pain, the love. You are infinite."*

They stood there, together, as the world continued to turn around them. Istanbul's lights flickered on, the calls of the evening echoed through the air, and the waves of the Bosphorus moved gently below. But for them, time stood still—an endless, timeless canvas yet to be filled.

With a deep breath, Aylin closed her journal and rested her head against Emir's chest, feeling the pulse of his life, the warmth of his presence. They had traveled through love, loss, and everything in between, and now, standing together, they knew that no matter what came next, they would face it with hearts open and brushes ready.

Because love, like art, was a journey—one that never truly ended, but simply changed with each new chapter.

*

PART 2

*"Sometimes, the deepest
connections are felt,
not spoken."*

Chapter 11

Whispers of Fate

"Let yourself be silently drawn by the strange pull of what you really love. It will not lead you astray." - Rumi

In the stillness of late afternoon, Liana sat at a small café overlooking the Bosphorus. The sun cast golden rays on the water, creating a shimmering dance of light that felt almost magical. Outside, the world seemed calm, but inside her heart, a storm brewed. Fresh from her trip to Turkey, memories swirled in her mind, and questions hung in the air like the scent of brewed coffee.

She was not alone in her deliberation. Across the table sat Joseph, a close friend through life's ups and downs. Inert smiles and innately comprehending airs toward her complicities soothed her during moments when words could not speak for themselves.

"What's bothering you, Liana?" Joseph said, sipping his coffee with firm but full-of-compassion eyes. *"You look elsewhere."*

In the memory of the time spent with Omer, intimate conversations that seemed to have fitted another world better, suddenly came alive before Liana. She remembered how she had thought of their time in Turkey, the landscapes and ancient history that surrounded them. But these images were incomplete without the last piece that would connect them to the real feelings that they had for one another.

"I just have this feeling," she said, her fingers tracing the brim of her cup. *"That there's something I'm missing, bigger than just ourselves."*

Joseph leaned in, fascinated. *"You're thinking of the interconnection between us, aren't you? How does that link us?"*

Liana nodded, remembering the poems of Rumi that had spoken to her soul. *"It is as if he said, 'The wound is the place where the Light enters you.' I feel something so profound is being taught through my wounds, yet I do not know what."*

Just then, a sudden din at the nearby table erupted. A group of tourists, energetic and animated, huddled together to discuss how they could delve deeper into the city for further exploration. Among the crowd, one tall woman with striking features and infectious energy drew Liana's attention.

"This city has secrets," exclaimed the woman, her hand in an impressive gesture. *"We have to find the hidden gems beyond the usual traps for tourists!"*

Intrigued, Liana leaned forward. Joseph followed her gaze, his expression in a display of amusement. *"Looks like someone's on a quest."*

"Perhaps she knows something," Liana said, a spark in her eyes. *"What if we joined them? It might be one way to discover something unexpected."*

After exchanging a few pleasantries, Liana and Joseph introduced themselves, and before they knew it, they were wrapped up in an enthusiastic discussion. The woman's name was Elif, a local artist with a taste for the mystical and bizarre. As she spoke of the wonders of this city that few people knew, her enthusiasm was contagious.

"You haven't been to Istanbul if you don't wander the streets of Balat," she said, her eyes sparkling. *"It's where past and present collide in the most beautiful chaos."*

The places yet to be visited thrilled Liana, feeling so alien to her heart and almost hankering after adventure.

As they wandered deeper into Balat, the sun began to set, casting a golden glow over the colored buildings lining the streets. Each one was a different story painted onto its canvas, its colors worn yet somehow alive with life. The energy of the city pulsed around Liana, intoxicating her.

"This street has been a witness to centuries," Elif said in a whisper, catching her breath as they turned a bend. *"Once upon a time, all kinds of different cultures were living here: Jews, Greeks, Armenians. Each turn, each house tells an ancient secret."*

Liana listened as her imagination began to develop a picture of how lives once pulsed in these streets. She couldn't help but feel that some thread, thrown through time, interconnected people in ways they hardly suspected.

"You can almost hear their voices if you listen closely," Joseph added, his eyes sparkling with curiosity. *"Like echoes of history still hanging in the air."*

The trio came upon an art gallery nestled between two old buildings. Its entrance was peculiarly designed with colorful mosaics. A board above the entrance said *"Eternal Whispers,"* and for some incomprehensible motive, Liana felt herself being pulled inside. The air was thick with creativity, as on each wall hung paintings to which life had been breathed into them, every canvas telling a different story.

Inside, it was full of the smell of turpentine, and soft music played. The owner greeted them from inside, an elderly man with wise eyes.

"Welcome to my sanctuary," he said, swinging his hand around to indicate the artwork. *"Every piece here carries the soul of an artist."*

The beauty that lay around her from every direction thrilled Liana's heart as they strolled along the gallery. Each piece was reaching some part of her being: an abstract capturing the chaos of emotion within her, a serene landscape echoing her longing for peace.

"Art has a way of saying what words can't," she mused aloud, her fingers brushing against a canvas depicting a sea of swirls. *"It's as if it shows us the truths within us that even we have never seen."*

"Exactly," Elif said, her enthusiasm contagious. *"It is an exact form of art-tongue, class, race. It puts us all into a circle that we cannot fully comprehend."*

Then, a small, delicate painting caught Liana's eye: A woman stood on the edge of a cliff, her hair blowing in the wind, gazing out at a sea that stretched to infinity. The colors were very soft and unreal; Liana felt a strong pang of longing.

"This piece is called 'The Edge of Dreams,'" the gallery owner explained as he approached. *"It represents the moment of choice—when one stands on the precipice of their destiny."*

Liana felt her heart racing as she absorbed the meaning behind the artwork. *"It's beautiful,"* she breathed, feeling like it told its tale directly to her journey—her struggles, her love for Omer, and her search for purpose.

"Could you tell me who the artist is?" she inquired curiously.

"A talented soul from the city," replied the owner, beaming with a smile. *"She captured in her work the sense of human emotion. She has since disappeared, leaving behind only rumors of her talent."*

Curiosity, the mystery, lit a fire within Liana. *"Do you think that's something I can find?"* she asked, wide-eyed with determination.

The owner of the gallery chuckled softly. *"The way you find an artist is just like the way you find inspiration; it's often running away from you when you chase it. But I can tell you where she was last seen."*

That small instance sparked an idea in Liana's mind—maybe she could find the story about the artist and perhaps draw parallels to her own. And with each passing moment, the idea bloomed in her heart, laced with her growing need for connection and understanding.

They continued into the evening, having street food and trying local snacks. They walked up to a vendor of simit, a sort of sesame-crusted bread ring, and laughed as they enjoyed the crunchiness of it.

"You have to try this with cheese," Joseph urged, having a great big bite. *"It's life-changing!"*

She watched him savor the taste as the radiance of his joy was infectious. *"Sometimes, it is the simple things in life that give us the most happiness,"* she said, taking one for herself and feeling the flavors explode in her mouth.

Deepening darkness found them on a rooftop that overlooked the glittering skyline of Istanbul: a city twinkling at every turn, an endless expanse of stars, every light a life, every light a story, every light a connection.
"Isn't it amazing?" Elif whispered, staring at the view. *"This city is alive with stories waiting to be discovered."*

Liana felt the peace wash over her, the chaos of her life momentarily stilled by beauty. *"It's magical,"* she said in agreement, her heart swelling with gratitude for the journey that had brought her here.

Suddenly, it dawned on her. *"Why not start a project?"* she burst forth excitedly. *"A combined artistic performance that could reveal the story of our very experiences—these journeys and connections."*

Elif's eyes lit up. *"That is brilliant! We will get stories from the locals, and each of us can add to our art and poetry."*

Joseph nodded in agreement. *"We could feature it in the gallery! This place needs to see the vibrancy of its community."*

The idea set fire to Liana. They spent the rest of the night discussing the project, sharing their visions and hopes, each one adding layers to the tapestry they were about to create.

For the first time in a very long time, Liana woke at dawn with a reason to be. This was so much more than an art project; this would interlink the strains of their lives, the stories of those around her, together with her journey.

"We'll call it 'Echoes of Connection,'" said Liana, with passion oozing from every word. *"A celebration of the unseen threads that bind us all."*

The others cheered, and together, they embraced the dawn of a new chapter in their lives.

In the stillness of night, fate softly calls,
With gentle whispers that weave through the halls.
Threads of tomorrow, in shadows they blend,
Guiding our journeys, where destinies bend.
A chance meeting here, a choice made there,
In the dance of our lives, fate's breath fills the air.

Listen closely, dear heart, to the signs that await,
For in every whisper, lies the echo of fate.

Back in Istanbul, meanwhile, Liana's mind wandered back to Omer, her heart, which was torn apart by the distance separating them. Would he understand this new passion, this new path she was taking? More importantly, would he be there when she got home?

She resolved to reach out to him, to share her newly awakened inspiration and the exciting project at hand. Liana took a deep breath. Her heart was filled with hope.

"Sometimes, it takes an away journey to find yourself very much inside," she whispered to herself, quoting Rumi. *"And in every journey, the heart speaks so loudly when words wouldn't be enough."*

The more Liana walked into her life with plans and visions, the more crystal clear her perspective became. This was no longer just a chapter of love or a chapter of loss; it became a story of finding one's voice, connecting with people, and rejoicing over the beauty of human existence.

She stood at the threshold, waiting to bloom amid Istanbul, where whispers of fate mingled with murmurs of the past into the light embrace of the unknown, to forge her path forward, one brush stroke at a time.

Chapter 12

The Path of Awakening

"Do not be satisfied with the stories that come before you. Unfold your own myth." — Rumi

Smack in the middle of Istanbul, a city bathed in layers of history and spirituality, Liana woke up that morning with a sense of determination humming in her veins, as if the universe had taken a direct interest in leading her further into the insight of herself and her connection to the world. She had an innate calling to understand not only the art of the city but also the soul's journey within the cosmic dance of creation.

Having had a healthy breakfast with Joseph and Elif, they decided to visit the Sultanahmet historic district with its famous sights.

The greatness of Hagia Sophia and the Blue Mosque astonished the heart of every traveler, yet Liana felt an urge deeper than just sightseeing; she craved a spiritual awakening.

As they walked toward the Hagia Sophia, its spacious dome towering above, Liana felt almost crushed by the weight of history. A basilica, then a mosque, now a museum—the purpose of the building had changed several times over the centuries. Each layer of its existence resonated with the prayers and hopes of countless souls. She remembered Rumi: *"The wound is the place where the Light enters you."*

"Liana, are you alright?" Joseph's voice pierced her reverie. *"You look as if you were in another world."*

Liana smiled dreamily, her eyes sparkling with emotion. *"I am, somehow. This space has so many stories; it is like a tapestry of faith and devotion."*

But alongside her admiration for the historical marvel, a wave of nostalgia washed over her. She recalled her last visit here with Omer, the way they had wandered through the halls hand in hand, marveling at the intricate mosaics and sharing whispers of their dreams. She remembered how he had spoken passionately about the building's transformation and its embodiment of resilience through time. The memory of his laughter and the warmth of his presence made her heart ache with longing. *"Omer would love this,"* she thought, a bittersweet smile touching her lips.

Elif nodded in agreement. *"This place is more than just architecture; it epitomizes the very essence of human connection through the divine."*

Inside Hagia Sophia, Liana felt herself wrapped in otherworldly serenity. The sunlight poured through the glass in jewel colors, casting colorful reflections against the marble floors and illuminating the sacred space. The air buzzed with reverence as visitors moved wordlessly, their whispers tumbling upon each other against the ancient walls.

"Look at the dome," Elif pointed, her voice barely above a whisper. *"It feels as though it is reaching out to the heavens."*
Liana followed her gaze to the incredibly intricate mosaics depicting biblical scenes. They spoke of a faith that time could not kill, a yearning to be reunited with the divine. The artistry was at once humbling and uplifting, a testament to humanity's quest for meaning.

Further in, as they made their way deeper into the building, Liana felt an inkling to step into a small alcove away from the jostling crowds. The atmosphere here was quiet, emotionally electric in the air, yet similarly ill-defined within her senses. She spotted a little wooden bench and sat down, closing her eyes to collect her thoughts.

The stillness enveloped her, and she breathed deeply, letting the echoes of the past wash over her. Each inhale felt like drawing in the spirit of those who had come before her, a collective breath shared among generations. With her eyes shut, she could almost hear the faint whispers of prayers long gone, the hopes and dreams woven into the very fabric of the walls surrounding her.

In that moment, Liana felt an overwhelming connection to everything—her past, her journey, her search for meaning, and even the unknown paths ahead. She recalled her recent conversations with Omer, their discussions on art and existence, the way he challenged her to see beyond the surface. *"What do you seek, Liana?"* a soft voice seemed to ask from within.

"I seek understanding," she whispered back, though she knew not if anyone could hear her. *"I want to know how I fit into this grand tapestry."*

The gentle light streaming through her eyelids began to intensify, filling her with warmth. It was as if the universe were reassuring her that she was part of something much larger than herself.

Moments later, Joseph's voice broke through her meditative state. *"Liana, are you coming?"* He beckoned her with a smile, unaware of the transformation she had just experienced.

Opening her eyes, Liana felt lighter, as if a veil had been lifted from her heart. *"Yes, I'm coming,"* she replied, her voice steadier than before.

As they left the alcove, the three friends explored the remainder of Hagia Sophia, each step feeling imbued with new meaning. The grand columns and vast arches no longer merely represented history; they echoed Liana's personal awakening.

Outside, the bustling sounds of Istanbul wrapped around them, yet Liana felt a serene sense of purpose. The beauty of the city now appeared richer, the colors more vibrant, as if she were seeing everything for the first time.

"What's next on our journey?" Elif asked, her eyes sparkling with enthusiasm.

"I think we should explore the local art scene," Liana suggested, her spirit ignited by her newfound insight. *"There's so much creativity waiting to be discovered."*

Joseph nodded in agreement. *"I'm all in! Let's uncover more stories."*

Together, they set off into the vibrant streets, their laughter mingling with the sounds of the city, each step echoing Liana's awakening. She could feel the threads of her connection to the world tightening, and her heart swelled with anticipation for what lay ahead.

As they wandered through hidden galleries and artisan shops, Liana felt as though she were gathering pieces of her soul, connecting not just with the art, but with the essence of each artist's journey. Every brushstroke, every sculpture, told a story that resonated within her, as if she were weaving her narrative into the larger tapestry of Istanbul.

"This is only the beginning," she thought, her heart brimming with possibilities. *"I will embrace every experience, every connection."*

Certainly! Here's the continuation of Liana's journey, connecting it to the previous narrative and incorporating italicized dialogue for clarity:

Liana felt the weight of her newfound understanding as she sat in the café, the fragrant aroma of coffee swirling around her. The vibrant atmosphere outside echoed her inner excitement. She reflected on the event they had just hosted, feeling the threads of connection woven between everyone who had come together.

"Connection is such a potent force; it cuts through time and space and even loss," she mused aloud, her pen dancing across the pages of her journal. *"I am finding, as I make this journey, that each happy or sad encounter in life gives richness to the tapestry that is our lives."*

Just then, Joseph joined her at the table, a warm smile lighting up his face. *"I've been thinking about what you said during the event,"* he began, leaning in. *"The way you described the bonds we share... it resonated with everyone."*

Liana smiled, feeling a sense of gratitude. *"I just spoke from my heart. This journey has shown me how we are all connected, and I wanted everyone to feel that."*

Elif soon arrived, her energy infectious. *"I heard someone talking about starting a community for artists and storytellers,"* she teased, a twinkle in her eye. *"I think we might have a movement on our hands!"*

Liana chuckled, her heart swelling with excitement. *"Imagine how beautiful it would be if we could create a space for everyone to share their stories, their art, and their lives. We could hold workshops, invite more artists, and even host open mic nights!"*
"It sounds perfect," Joseph said, nodding enthusiastically. *"This city is brimming with talent, and we can be the bridge that connects those who wish to share their voices."*

Liana took a deep breath, envisioning the possibilities. *"We could even include themed events, like one dedicated to exploring grief and healing through art. Just like Aylin's story, which deserves to be heard."*

Elif leaned closer, her voice filled with passion. *"Yes! We could help others find solace in sharing their pain and joy. It could be a safe haven for everyone."*

As the three friends brainstormed ideas, Liana felt a wave of inspiration wash over her. Each suggestion sparked another, and soon, they were planning for their next event, their excitement infectious.

"This is just the beginning," she said, her heart racing with anticipation. *"We can create a community that celebrates life in all its forms, where stories bind us together."*

Days turned into weeks as they organized meetings, reached out to local artists, and cultivated a network of storytellers eager to join their cause. Liana immersed herself in this new mission, her journal becoming a treasure trove of ideas and reflections.

One evening, she found herself at a quiet spot in the park where she had first met the elderly man. The cherry blossoms were in bloom again, their delicate petals dancing in the breeze. As she sat under the tree, she opened her journal, her thoughts flowing freely.

"Life is a collection of stories, woven together like threads in a beautiful tapestry. Each connection we forge adds depth to our existence, shaping us in ways we may never fully comprehend."

In that moment, Liana felt the presence of the old man beside her. She could almost hear his voice echoing in her mind. *"Time is priceless. Live to the fullest, love deeply, and cherish every single moment."*

Determined to honor that wisdom, Liana dedicated herself to this journey of connection, knowing that with every story shared, they would weave a vibrant community, a tapestry rich in love, loss, and everything in between.

And as the next event approached, anticipation filled the air. Liana could sense the growing momentum, the collective heartbeat of a community ready to embrace the beauty of storytelling.

"Together," she whispered to herself, *"we will create something extraordinary."*

"Maybe next we could work on love," *Elif suggested, her voice ringing with enthusiasm. "Not just the love between romantic partners but also the love between friends, family, and communities."*

Liana felt a spark of excitement as her imagination took flight. *"Yes! Each type has its own story to tell, and I believe this will bring people together in wonderful ways."*

As they left the hall, Liana sensed the universe gently nudging them forward. She felt a growing conviction that she needed to pursue this journey of exploration, eager to learn how they could share their stories and create something truly beautiful together.

In the days that followed, Liana often reflected on the wisdom shared by the elderly man in the park.

"Life is indeed a tapestry," she mused as she wandered through the bustling streets of Istanbul, a city pulsing with life. Every encounter and fleeting moment wove itself into the fabric of their lives. The echoes of laughter and the tantalizing scents of spices filled the air, reminding her of the community she was nurturing.

Thus began the planning for the next live event, an exhilarating endeavor that filled her with purpose. Liana stood at the cusp of something transformative, a movement ready to deepen the bonds among those she cherished. She jotted down her thoughts in her journal:

"What is love?" she wrote. *"It can be both joyful and painful, transformative. It can bind us and yet shatter us. I want to explore how love shapes our identities and guides our paths, and how it unites us in profound ways. We must embrace this essential part of our humanity and celebrate it."*

Liana decided to incorporate various forms of expression, including music, poetry, visual arts, and storytelling. She reached out to local artists, poets, and musicians, inviting them to share their interpretations of love.

As the date approached, anticipation surged within her, a mixture of excitement and anxiety. She was determined to craft an experience that resonated with everyone, travelers on the magnificent journey of love. Teary-eyed and heart racing, she arrived early on the day of the event.

A charming courtyard sparkled with twinkling fairy lights, colorful drapes fluttering in the breeze. Artists were setting up installations while the sounds of guitar strumming and instrumental tuning melded into a lively symphony.

"Liana! Look at this!" Elif exclaimed, her enthusiasm bubbling over as she unveiled a large canvas. It revealed an abstract swirling rendering of love's colors, dancing in a tangle that mirrored the beautifully complex nature of human relationships.

"This is beautiful, Elif!" Liana exclaimed, her eyes wide with awe. *"You've captured love so vividly."*

Elif beamed, her cheeks flushed with pride. *"I wanted to show that love can be chaotic yet breathtaking all at once; it can uplift us and sometimes bring us down."*

As the event commenced, Liana welcomed her guests with a radiant smile. The courtyard filled with individuals of all ages, each carrying their stories and life experiences. A sense of warmth enveloped Liana as familiar faces mingled with newcomers, creating an atmosphere rich with possibility.

"Tonight, we come together to explore love in all its facets," Liana began, her voice steady yet full of emotion. *"We are here to share stories, art, and music—each an expression of our diverse experiences, adding to the beautiful tapestry of our existence. Let us open our hearts and allow the beauty of love to envelop us in its myriad forms."*

The evening unfolded in a cascade of performances and presentations. Poets recited poignant verses on the pangs of lost love, the joy of new beginnings, and the unbreakable bonds of friendship. Musicians played soulful melodies, harmonizing with the emotions that filled the crowd.

As Liana moved among the guests, she overheard snippets of conversation, bursts of laughter, and intimate moments. Strangers were sharing their lives, weaving their stories into the vibrant fabric of the evening.

"This is what it's all about," she whispered to herself, her spirit soaring.

When Aylin took the stage, Liana felt a surge of anticipation. The artist approached with trembling hands.

"I'd like to share a piece I created after losing someone very dear to me," Aylin began, her voice soft yet steady. *"It's about love that transcends death."*

As Aylin unveiled her painting—a hauntingly beautiful depiction of flowers blossoming from the shadows—an awed silence fell over the audience.

"For love does not fade with loss; it transforms. It becomes a part of us. This garden represents the change it has brought to my life," Aylin continued, her eyes shimmering with unshed tears. *"There is still beauty, hope, and love to be found behind the veil of grief."*

The audience erupted into applause, and a deep resonance stirred within Liana as Aylin spoke. It was a powerful reminder that love endures beyond loss. As the night unfolded, Liana watched as friendships blossomed, stories unfolded, and hearts opened.

As the event drew to a close, Liana felt a profound sense of fulfillment. She embraced Elif and Joseph, three friends basking in the glow of a successful evening.

"This was magic," Joseph said, his tone overflowing with joy. *"You created such a wonderful space for people to share their hearts."*

"And heal," Elif added, her voice full of warmth. *"I can feel the energy here."*

Liana's heart swelled with pride. *"It's all about building relationships through our stories. We must keep this journey alive."*

After the event, Liana reflected on what had transpired. She opened her journal and began to write:

"It is love that binds us, joy that elevates us, sorrow that teaches us, and experiences that unite us. By sharing our stories, we can cultivate communities rooted in empathy, kindness, and our shared humanity. This is a theme I want to explore further, delving into the nuances of love and our connections."

For months, Liana continued her work, organizing events that touched on various themes of love: romantic love, familial ties, and the bonds of friendship. Each gathering unveiled new stories and deeper relationships, as her journey of self-discovery intertwined with the narratives of others.

One day, while wandering through a local park, Liana encountered the old man from the first event. His presence exuded a comfortable reassurance about her path.

"Hello, my dear," he said, his voice warm like sunlight breaking through clouds. *"It's good to see you again."*

"I've been reflecting on your words," Liana replied with a smile. *"How each interaction shapes us."*

"Indeed," he nodded. *"Every person you meet can alter your journey. Cherish those moments; they are fleeting."*

That afternoon, Liana sat beneath the cherry blossom trees, watching the petals dance in the gentle breeze like whispered secrets of the universe. She felt profoundly in tune with the world; each bloom imparted lessons on the beauty of impermanence.

Her heart knew she was on a quest to fathom the depths of love. Liana began weaving her experiences into her storytelling, exploring themes of vulnerability, trust, and the power of human bonds. As time passed and seasons changed, Liana's events gained momentum, attracting diverse voices and stories. Each meeting became a celebration of love's many manifestations—through art, laughter, tears, and shared experiences. One night, as she prepared for an open-mic gathering, a young woman approached her, urgency evident in her eyes. *"I heard about your gatherings, and I want to share my story,"* she said, her voice trembling with passion.

"We'd love to hear it," Liana encouraged, her heart swelling with admiration for the woman's bravery. *"Your story matters."*

Listeners held their breath as the young woman poured her heart out, recounting tales of love and heartbreak. The audience was spellbound, absorbing every word; the palpable energy in the room ebbed and flowed with the rhythm of her emotions. Later, Liana approached the young woman, her eyes sparkling with gratitude. *"Thank you for sharing your story. It takes incredible courage to be so open."*

"I owe my gratitude to you for creating this space," she replied, her voice thick with emotion. *"Sometimes, I don't realize what I'm holding onto until moments like tonight."*

As weeks turned into months, Liana became deeply woven into her community. Each interaction enriched her spirit, transforming her journey of self-discovery into a collective healing experience.

One evening, as she reflected on the events that had unfolded, she wrote in her journal:

"I firmly believe this is a moment where my experiences intertwine with those I encounter. It is the journey, the weaving of a tapestry ever-changing, filled with joys and sorrows, bonds formed and broken. Every story shared strengthens the ties that bind us. I am learning that this vulnerability is not a weakness but a strength that fosters intimacy and understanding. We come together to create community: our narratives matter."

Beneath the starry Istanbul sky, Liana crafted her tapestry of experiences, line by line, each thread reflecting the transformative power of love. Gazing out into the bustling city, she felt a deep sense of purpose. She was ready to embrace whatever came next, knowing that every encounter would further illuminate her path.

And so, the journey continued—a journey of love and stories, of beautiful threads uniting them all. Liana understood that life was interwoven into a mosaic of shared experiences, each golden moment reminding her of the myriad relationships that shape their existence. With this last note, she closed her journal for that night and said a silent prayer of thanks. The path ahead was still unraveling, but this much she knew for certain: She was right where she was meant to be, embracing the journey, ready to explore deeply the capacity of love and connection and humanness.

Chapter 13

The Dance of Love and Light

"Love is the bridge between you and everything. Dance, when you're broken open. Dance, if you've torn the bandage off. Dance in the middle of the fighting. Dance in your blood. Dance when you're perfectly free." - Rumi

The dawn breaking over Istanbul, casting gold off the Bosphorus, found Liana wakeful and ready. Energy still buzzed in her veins, heated by the gathering around the passion for storytelling and simply connecting. Deep inside, she yearned to plunge into all the various facets of love, its beauty and its problems, and the wisdom it bestows.

She'd spent her morning in the comfort of her studio, surrounded by canvases and paintbrushes, with the fresh aroma of brewed coffee. The sun shone through the window, casting its warmth into the room. She opened her journal and wrote:

Today, I want to discuss the dance of love and light. Love is not just a feeling; it is a movement that sometimes teaches and, at times, even tests our will. It is a dance, a rhythm we learn to move toward as time goes along. I want to find out how love lights the way and what lessons are learned in the darkness.

As she wrote, images flooded back to Liana: the moments of joy that had made her heart soar, the heartaches that had taught her about resilience. She reflected on her relationships: her deep bond with Omer, her cherished friendship with Joseph, and the beautiful connections she had forged through her events.

Her mind strayed to the old gentleman she met in the park, whose words of wisdom still lingered in her heart. She remembered his saying that every encounter shapes our journey, love is stitched through loss, and every story shared adds depth to the understanding of humanity.

That afternoon, Liana prepared a mini gathering at her studio, where she invited her close friends and other artists to share the theme of love through their various artistic expressions. She wanted to create an intimate space where vulnerability was embraced and stories flowed freely.

When her friends finally arrived, the air was abuzz with excitement. Omer came with a guitar, Elif with a pile of her works, and Joseph with a poetry-filled notebook. The warmth of camaraderie enveloped them instantly, their hearts swelling with thanks.

"I am so glad you all could come. Tonight we are going to speak of love in all its forms: through music, through art, through stories. Let's weave a tapestry of expressions that reflect our experiences," Liana said.

They began with songs, starting with Omer softly playing his guitar as they sat in a circle. The sound waltzed in the air, wrapping them into its gentle hold. Every note was blanketed with the theme of love, bringing back memories and evoking emotions within them.

"This song is all about the beauty of falling in love," Omer said, his voice filled with warmth as he sang. The lyrics conveyed joy, the excitement of new beginnings, and Liana's heart fluttered with nostalgia, thinking of her moments of infatuation and the blissful uncertainty those moments carried.

After Omer, Elif went ahead and showed them her paintings, each canvas a different dimension of love in itself: one dancing couple under the stars, another child embracing a parent with a bond of warmth and security.

"This piece is about the love of friends," Elif explained, pointing at a painting of hands clasped together, fingertips touching lightly. *"Friendship is a dance in beautiful motion—a balance between trusting and understanding. It feeds the soul and picks us up when we go down."*

These words of Elif stirred something deep within Liana. She knew well how, more often than not, friendship intertwined itself with love, forming a beautiful tapestry of consolation and understanding.

Now, it was Joseph's turn. He stood up, clasping his notebook in his hand. *"I've written a poem,"* he said, his voice firm and steady. *"It's about the ambiguities of love—it can raise us yet wound us."*

As he spoke his poem, Liana was jolted by the weight of emotion woven into every word. He spoke about the beauty of love entwined with pain, how he learned his lessons through heartache, and the resilience that love fosters.

"Love is a journey of growth," Joseph summed up, his voice filled with conviction. *"It teaches us to embrace vulnerability and to cherish the moments that define us."*

When Joseph had finished, a contemplative silence fell in the room, as if each of the friends remembered the strength of love, its beauty, and its lessons. The atmosphere brimmed with understanding as their thoughts were shared, Liana's heart opening wider.

"I believe love also calls us to forgive," she added, her voice cutting through the silence. *"Forgiveness is a gift we give ourselves, allowing us to release the burdens that hold us back."*

"Exactly," Omer interjected. *"When we forgive, we free ourselves to love more fully. It's a vital part of the dance."*

As the night wore on, the mood shifted. They spoke of love lost and love found, each story unraveling the intricacies of their lives. Laughter and tears wove a rich brocade of emotions, each tender moment stitched into their shared experience.
It was as if the walls of her studio had transformed into a sacred space, barely containing the resonance vibrating through them. The more they shared, the deeper their understanding of love seemed to grow.

Later that evening, when it was time for one final reflection together, Liana could not help but express her gratitude. *"Thank you all for opening your hearts tonight,"* she said warmly. *"This gathering reminded me again of the importance of these bonds and how beautiful it is to share in each other's life experiences. Love is, indeed, a dance—a delicate balance of light and shadow."*

"And we're all learning the steps together," Elif added, a sparkle in her eyes. *"We each bring a different rhythm to this dance, making it significant for everyone."*

Liana smiled, her heart full. *"I'd like to continue creating space for these themes to be explored together. Let's not wait for the next event; let's keep the conversation going."*

Over the next few weeks, Liana's studio transformed into a haven where her friends were welcomed to share their stories and delve into the boundless dimensions of love. Regular meetings contemplated one form of love or another—romantic, platonic, familial, and self—one at a time.

The described acts of storytelling, creating art, and playing music inspired her. She started putting them into her journal, weaving all these into a collective narrative of what this journey meant for all of them together.

Reflecting on the evening's feeling made Liana sit in her studio and consider some of the wisdom she had learned:

"Love is a dance between light and dark; it teaches us to wear our vulnerability, treasure the bonds that bind us, and forgive. Each story that has been shared has been another thread sewn into the tapestry of our lives. I'm learning that the beauty of love does not lie just in joy, but in the way, it shapes and connects us in its complexity."

As months flowed into seasons, Liana witnessed her life blossom in ways she had never quite imagined. Her meetings grew in number and significance, drawing people from every walk of life. They shared their stories, their art, and their songs, weaving a rich tapestry of shared experiences.

One evening, after a particularly stirring gathering, Liana stood on her balcony, awed by the glittering lights of Istanbul. It was a city alive with possibility, with every light symbolizing a connection she had fostered.

Liana's heart was full to bursting, and a silent prayer of thanks escaped her lips: *"Thank you for the love that enfolds us, for the stories binding us, and for the continuing journey."* For Liana, every new day was a new way to explore the depth of love, create relationships, and weave her story into the fabric of life.

Thus, the journey continued—a dance of love and light, wherein with every step taken, she understood that human connections were boundless.

Chapter 14

Echoes of Solitude

In the echo of solitude, the heart speaks its quietest truths, and in that stillness, we learn to listen to the voice we often silence."

The sun was setting, casting a soft light over Istanbul, and Liana found herself wandering along the narrow streets of her district. The air was filled with the rich aroma of spices and the distant sounds of street musicians. Yet, despite the vibrant surroundings, a profound sense of loneliness weighed heavily on her heart, like a thick fog enveloping her.

There are times in life when we are surrounded by so many and yet feel so alone, she whispered to herself, recalling the words of

Rumi: *"The wound is the place where the Light enters you."* The echoes of her past tugged at her heartstrings, drawing her deeper into contemplation.

Liana's gatherings had transformed into a sanctuary of sorts, yet amid the laughter, bonding, and tears of joy, she felt a lingering void within her. It was as if her soul craved something deeper, a connection that transcended mere surface interactions—a yearning to make sense of love and loss. She stood on the edge of understanding something profound yet struggled to grasp its essence.

One evening, following a particularly joyous gathering, Liana retreated to her studio, unable to shake the bittersweet memories that hung in the air. She picked up her journal and began to write:

What is love if not a two-edged sword that can take us to the highest highs and plunge us deep into despair? It is in those moments of bliss that we forget how love can hurt. Yet, it is often through that pain that we find ourselves anew.

That night, a heavy melancholy settled over her. A torrent of unspoken thoughts weighed upon her as she gazed out at the city's shimmering lights. She remembered an elderly man in the park once telling her about the cyclical nature of love and loss: *"To love is to risk loss, but it is also to invite joy into our lives,"* he had said.

A tear slipped down Liana's cheek, tracing a path along her jawline. She had loved deeply in her life—especially Omer, whose presence had colored her world in shades of warmth and light. Yet, with each connection, her heart felt the sharp sting of anxiety, ever aware that everything in life was temporary, fragile, and often fleeting.

"Love is the whisper that doesn't last," she wrote, *"a gentle stroke that may vanish in an instant. When we hold on too tightly, we suffocate that which we wish to preserve."* The words poured from her heart like a river, each line reflecting her inner turmoil.

She sank into her reverie, recalling those moments of isolation where she floated on a sea of emotions. During those times, poetry often became her refuge—a catharsis for her pain.

"In solitude, I find clarity," she wrote. *"In the stillness of my heart, I hear echoes of my soul. It is here that I confront my fears, my hopes, and the fragility of existence. I am learning that it is in these quiet moments that the most profound truths reveal themselves."*

As the night deepened, Liana felt a powerful urge to be enveloped by the warmth of friends. Perhaps their company would provide the solace she sought. She made her way to Omer's apartment, a place where nights filled with music and laughter were a regular occurrence.

Upon entering, she was greeted by a jovial atmosphere. Omer strummed his guitar lightly, his fingers dancing across the strings, filling the air with the familiar melodies that echoed with camaraderie. But as she took a seat in a corner, she felt a distance grow between herself and the others. She observed their laughter and carefree dancing, their energy radiating around her like a vibrant tapestry, contrasting sharply with the stillness inside her.

"Liana!" Omer called out, his face brightening with a smile that always had the power to lift her spirits. *"Come join us! We'd love to have you!"*

She forced a smile, though the weight in her chest remained unyielding. Instead of joining the festivities, she sank deeper into her corner, an outsider gazing in at the warmth of connection around her—a stark reminder of the joy she longed to embrace but felt unable to.

As the evening progressed, Liana yearned for meaningful conversation, something real that would break through the superficiality that often clouded their gatherings. *Why do we gather if not to share something authentic?* she pondered, restlessness bubbling within her.

With newfound resolve, she stood and cleared her throat, catching the attention of her friends. *"Could we take a moment?"* The music faded, and they turned to her with expressions of curiosity. *"I don't know about you, but I've been reflecting a lot on love, loss, and the complexities of our relationships. I need to speak my mind about something that's been weighing heavily on my heart."*

Omer's eyes softened with understanding as he set his guitar aside. *"We're here for you, Liana. Please, share your thoughts."*

Taking a deep breath, Liana began to speak, her voice steady yet tinged with vulnerability. *"Love is a beautiful paradox. It can elevate us to unimaginable heights, yet it can also plunge us into darkness. I often find myself caught between joy and sorrow, yearning for deeper connections while simultaneously fearing the pain of loss."*

Her words flowed freely, enveloping her friends in a tapestry of shared emotions. They listened in silence, their eyes reflecting understanding as she spoke of the moments when, despite being surrounded by friends, she felt achingly alone, how love could be both a blessing and a burden.

"In our quest for love," she continued, *"we often forget that its very foundation lies in vulnerability. We must dare to expose our hearts, even if that means risking pain. It is through that pain, however, that we grow."*

With every word, Liana felt the weight on her heart lighten. Her friends nodded, their expressions mirroring her sentiments as they began to share their own experiences: heartbreak, elation, and the complexities that love had brought into their lives.

"It's in these moments of vulnerability that we truly find connection," Joseph whispered. *"We all have our struggles, yet sharing them reminds us that we're not alone."*

As they exchanged stories, Liana felt a flicker of hope ignite within her, a reminder that love, in all its forms, was a risk worth taking. The atmosphere shifted, growing more intimate with every shared tale, as they embraced the complexities of their lives together.

Later that night, as the chatter began to quiet, Omer picked up his guitar once more. *"This song is for all of us,"* he said softly, strumming a gentle melody that wrapped around them like a warm embrace. Music filled the room, its rhythm echoing the sense of belonging that enveloped them.

Liana closed her eyes, surrendering to the moment. It was then she realized that love, while fraught with challenges, was a rich tapestry woven from the threads of shared experiences, laughter, and sorrow. The colors of their stories blended seamlessly, creating a masterpiece of life that would see them through.

As the night drew to a close, Liana felt rejuvenated, her spirit lifted. Though moments of loneliness still lingered, she was no longer alone. The echoes of her heart whispered reminders that love, even in its most painful forms, was a path worth traversing. Returning home that night, Liana felt lighter than she had in days. She opened her journal and wrote:

"In the rhythm between love and solitude, I find my step. I am learning to let the light in, allowing the shadows to shape the core of my being. To love is not merely an emotion; it is a process through which we are all intertwined."

And so, Liana continued along her path, discovering beauty in vulnerability, richness in her friendships, and strength in embracing both joy and sorrow. Each step brought her closer to the understanding of those deep-seated facets of human experience intertwined with love, loss, and the soul's gentle whispers. In the depths of her heart, Liana knew that Omer held a special place, and as she navigated her emotions, it became increasingly clear that her love for him was woven into the very fabric of her being.

Chapter 15

The Weight of Fate

Rumi once said:

"Try not to resist the changes that come your way. Instead, let life live through you. And do not worry that your life is turning upside down. How do you know that the side you are used to is better than the one to come?"

The air was tight with palpable tension as Liana woke up the following morning. The sun was up, but it was dull and gray, casting an almost otherworldly light in her studio. The events of the previous night lingered in her mind—moments shared in vulnerability—a bittersweet reminder of the love-and-loss balancing scale.

She stepped out onto her balcony, the familiar views of Istanbul greeting her. The city was alive, yet unease settled in the pit of her stomach. Perhaps it was the heaviness of their conversations from the night before, the brutal honesty and unguarded emotions. Or perhaps it was something else altogether, an instinctual awareness that her world was about to shift.

Later that afternoon, Liana joined Joseph for coffee in their out-of-the-way café, tucked into a nook of the bustling city. As they sat sipping drinks, dappled sunlight filtered through the leaves, but today, something about Joseph's demeanor hinted at an undercurrent of sorrow.

"You seem distant today," she said, frowning. *"Is everything alright?"*

Joseph huffed, his gaze drifting out to the street. *"I got some disturbing news last night. My father... he has been diagnosed with a serious illness."*

The words hung in the air like a dark cloud. Empathy washed through Liana in waves. *"Oh, Joseph, I am so sorry. What does that mean for you and your family?"*

"It's complicated," he replied, his voice thick with emotion. *"We're still waiting for more information, but the doctors say it's advanced. My family is in an uproar, and I feel so helpless."*

Liana leaned across the table, gently placing her hand over his. *"You're not helpless. You have people who care about you. We'll face this together."*

He nodded, but his eyes reflected a different story, bright with unshed tears. *"I'm scared of losing him, Liana. He's been my rock, my guiding light. The thought of him not being there... it's devastating."*

The weight of his words landed in her chest, resonating with the losses she had so dreaded. They sat in silence, the jingling of the café fading into the background as they shared in the grief weaving itself into the fabric of their lives.

As days passed, Joseph's father began to deteriorate. Each day spent in the hospital felt like a psychological seesaw, with flashes of hope amidst gut-wrenching despair. Liana stood by Joseph's side, his anchor, as he struggled through the grieving of an impending loss. They would sit for hours in silence, reading Rumi's poetry to console themselves, attempting to make sense of their pain.

"When the soul lies down in that grass, the world is too full to talk about; ideas, language, even the phrase 'each other' doesn't make

any sense,'" she read one evening in a soft tone, looking up to find Joseph's eyes brimming with tears.

"Rumi always seems to know how to capture what I feel," he whispered. The ache was etched upon his face, pain evident in his eyes. *"But even his words don't seem to ease this heaviness in my heart."*

It was a fateful evening, shrouded in eerie silence, when they sat together in his father's hospital room. The air felt tense, thick with unspoken words. Joseph's father lay fragile in bed, yet his presence remained so strong in many ways. Slowly, he opened his eyes, recognizing both Liana and his son.

"You have come to see me, my boy," he whispered, barely audible. *"Always, Dad,"* Joseph replied, his voice breaking as he fought back tears. *"I'm here. We're both here."*

Liana felt an overwhelming surge of emotion tugging at her heartstrings. She clung to Joseph's hand, offering him her strength in a moment that demanded so much of them.

"I want you to know," Joseph's father continued, locking eyes with each of them, *"that the greatest gifts of all are those of love given and received. These are what count at the very end: memories and contact."*

These words resonated deeply with Liana. In his vulnerability, she sensed profound wisdom; there was an unspoken truth hanging in the air—a preciousness to this moment, this touch.

Time wore on, the room filled with shared tales and bittersweet laughter—a celebration of love and life. Joseph's father recounted stories from his childhood, moments filled with joy, laughter, and even heartache. Liana listened intently, absorbing every word as if they were golden threads weaving a tapestry of legacy.

But as the evening progressed, the mood shifted. The beeping of the machines became more steady, an honest reminder of the fragility of the thread between life and death. Joseph's father struggled for breath, and a chill gripped Liana's heart.

Suddenly, the monitors began to beep wildly. Joseph leapt to his father's side, panic etched across his features. *"Dad! Stay with us!"* His voice broke, drowning in dread.

Tears streamed down Liana's face as she stood silently, a feeling of helplessness crushing her chest. Time stretched, every second an eternity filled with unbearable fear.

In that agonizing moment, Joseph's father looked up at him, his eyes welling with tears. *"Remember, Joseph, love remains forever,"* he whispered. *"I will always be with you."*

Chaos erupted in the room as the machines flatlined. Liana felt her heart shatter as Joseph collapsed to his knees, overwhelmed by the pain of his loss. Everything blurred around them: the laughter and stories fell to an eerie silence.

Liana threw herself at his side as he, for the first time, wept beneath the weight of grief. *"I'm here. I'm here,"* she whispered, her voice shaking. *"You're not alone."*

But even as she spoke those words, her fears began seeping in, shrouding her in shadows. The reality of loss—a void left behind—served as a chilling reminder that life is fleeting.

In the days that followed, sorrow lay heavily between Liana and Joseph. The funeral was a gathering of somber faces, tears, and tales of a life well lived. Joseph's father had touched many lives, and in the bittersweet memories shared, Liana felt the beauty and fragility of connection.

"Life is fragile," she wrote in her diary that night, reflecting on the day's events. *"We are but echoes in the wind, leaving traces in the hearts of loved ones. The tragedy of loss is immeasurable, yet from that very loss, we are taught to cherish every moment."*

Liana remained by Joseph's side through the weeks and months that followed, her heart aching for him. She watched as the ache of loss deepened into a profound understanding of love's polyvalent nature—heartache intertwined with resilience.

"One finds in grief a strength," she said one evening as they sat on the balcony, overlooking the city. *"We learn to carry with us the love of those we have lost and allow that love to shape our lives."*

Joseph nodded, the shadows giving way to a flicker of hope in his eyes. *"You're right. Maybe I lost my father, but his love will stay with me, and it will always live on. That's what I carry forward."*

With that, they began to live in memory of his father, embracing life fully. They cherished moments of joy amidst sorrow and reminded each other of the beauty in their fragile, intertwined existence.

One night, Liana wrote in her journal, *"Love is our greatest legacy. It is the thread that weaves our separate stories together. Tragedy cannot snuff out the light of love that remains."*

Joseph's father had always embodied a paternal presence in their lives, a figure of strength and wisdom that filled a void they all shared; in many ways, he had become a surrogate father to them all. As orphans of different circumstances—Liana and Omer carrying the weight of familial absence, Joseph grappling with the impending loss of his only remaining parent—they found solace in the love and guidance he provided. He had nurtured their spirits, instilled values of compassion and resilience, and created a sense of belonging in a world that often felt cold and unforgiving. His laughter and warmth reminded them that even in the absence of blood relations, they were bound together by a tapestry of shared experiences, and it was through his love that they had learned the importance of family, however it was defined.

Joseph's father's funeral felt like a desolate landscape to all of them. Each morning began with a weight in their chests, a constant reminder of the void left behind not just for Joseph, but for all of them as well. In the depths of their heart, they felt a profound sense of loss, almost as if they were mourning their own biological father.

As the sun rose over Istanbul, casting pale light across her studio, Liana felt the shadows lengthening around her. The city was alive, bustling with life, yet within her, a deep sense of isolation took root. She recalled moments spent with Joseph's father—his laughter, his wisdom, and the warmth he had always extended. It was as if a part of her had been extinguished, leaving behind a chilling emptiness.

Daisy, their playful friend, had become quieter in the wake of the tragedy. Her laughter, once bright and infectious, now seemed dulled, echoing softly in the corners of their shared memories. *"It's hard to believe he's really gone,"* she whispered one evening as they gathered in Liana's studio, the weight of grief heavy in the air. *"I keep expecting him to walk through the door and ask us what we're up to, you know?"*

Liana nodded, tears pooling in her eyes. *"I keep waiting for that too, Daisy. It feels surreal, like a bad dream I can't wake up from. He was a guiding light in all our lives."*

Joseph sat in silence, his gaze distant, as if he were searching for his father in the memories that filled the room. Omer, sensing the palpable tension, reached out to him. *"You don't have to go through this alone, Joseph. We're here for you. Always."*

But the words felt inadequate. The bonds of friendship, though strong, seemed frail against the enormity of loss. Liana felt the tears she had been holding back spill over, and she quickly wiped them away, not wanting to show her vulnerability. Yet the truth was that each tear was a testament to the love they all held for Joseph's father, a man whose presence had knitted them together.

In the stillness of the night, Liana found herself alone on her balcony, looking out over the city she loved and the memories that now felt so bittersweet. She remembered the warmth of Joseph's father's embrace, the wisdom he shared, and the laughter they had all enjoyed. The grief settled heavily on her shoulders, an anchor that threatened to pull her under.

"Why does it hurt so much?" she murmured to the night. *"Why is the absence of one person enough to dim the light in so many lives?"* The silence around her offered no answers, only the echo of her sorrow.

One afternoon, as they sat in a café bathed in soft sunlight, Liana felt the need to speak up, to acknowledge the grief that had become a silent companion in their lives. *"I think we need to talk about what we're feeling,"* she said, her voice trembling. *"This pain... it's not something we should carry alone."*

Daisy looked up, her eyes glistening. *"I'm scared,"* she admitted, her voice barely above a whisper. *"Scared that we'll forget him, that the memories will fade, and that he'll be just another face in the crowd."*

Liana reached across the table, squeezing Daisy's hand. *"We won't forget him. We can keep his memory alive. We can share our stories, our moments with him, so he's never truly gone."*

Omer nodded in agreement, his expression somber. *"He taught us to love fiercely. We owe it to him to keep living, to keep our hearts open. He wouldn't want us to lose ourselves in sorrow."*

As they spoke, Joseph sat quietly, tears streaming down his cheeks. Liana's heart ached for him, knowing he carried a weight that was impossible to comprehend. *"You're not alone, Joseph,"* she said softly. *"We are all here, walking this painful path together."*

But even as she spoke, Liana felt the flicker of love for Omer stir within her—a confusing mix of grief and yearning. Omer's strength drew her in, yet the sadness that bound them all kept her at a distance, unsure of how to navigate the complexity of her emotions.

Days turned into weeks, and the world continued to move forward, but Liana felt as though she were stuck in a still frame, haunted by memories of loss. On particularly difficult days, she would sit with Omer on her balcony, sharing quiet moments, their silence filled with an understanding that needed no words. The connection between them deepened, yet she could not shake the guilt of finding solace in Omer when Joseph needed her the most.

One evening, as the sun set in a blaze of orange and purple, Liana turned to Omer, her voice cracking. *"I miss him so much, Omer. I wish I could just talk to him one more time, hear his voice, see his smile. It's like a piece of my heart is missing."*

Omer looked at her with a depth of understanding. *"I know, Liana. I miss him too. But we carry his love with us, in everything we do. It's in our laughter, our tears, and the moments we share. We have to keep him alive in our hearts."*

That night, Liana wrote in her journal, pouring her heart out. *"Grief is a heavy cloak that we wear, but it is also a reminder of the love we had. In the shadows of sorrow, we find pieces of light— memories that spark joy even in the darkest of times. We are not alone; we have each other, and through our shared pain, we can heal."*

As the ink dried, Liana felt a flicker of hope igniting within her—a reminder that love could flourish even amidst sorrow. She took a deep breath, knowing that while the road ahead would be difficult, they would walk it together, bound by the memories of a man who had taught them the true meaning of love and connection. And in doing so, perhaps they would find a way to carry the light of his memory forward, illuminating the shadows of their grief.

Chapter 16

The Echo of Light and Shadow

"The brighter the light, the deeper the shadows." – Rumi

Liana sat in her studio in the stillness of the early morning, where soft light filtered through the curtains. The quiet times had become increasingly appreciated for the soothing whispers from the world outside, balmy to her soul. This was vibrant Istanbul—whereas the heaviness clung to her heart like a shadow, she knew that both beauty and grief were inextricably linked: life and death.

She sipped her tea and turned to her journal, where she had been chronicling musings on mortality. *"Death,"* she wrote, *"is not an end but a transformation, a transition from one state of being to another."* The words flowed from her pen like a river of reflection, each line a testament to her evolving insight into the transient nature of life.

Later that evening, they gathered on the rooftop of their favorite café as the sun began to set, painting the sky orange and pink. Liana, Omer, Joseph, and Daisy sat together, sipping tea and sharing stories, yet the weight of their recent loss hung in the air like a thick fog.

"You've all been quiet lately," Liana said, glancing around at her friends. *"It feels like we're all lost in our thoughts."*

Omer looked away, tracing the horizon with his eyes. *"I've been thinking about what it means to live and die. It's hard to wrap my mind around it."* He paused, his voice heavy with emotion. *"One moment someone is so alive, and then... just gone."*

Joseph nodded, his gaze distant. *"It's terrifying. I keep wondering how we're supposed to go on without them."*

Daisy leaned forward, her expression earnest. *"What if death isn't about ending but changing forms?"* She looked at Liana, encouraging her to share her thoughts.

"Exactly," Liana replied, grateful for Daisy's support. *"Rumi said, 'The wound is the place where the Light enters you.' Maybe our experiences of loss are opportunities for deeper understanding."*

Omer's brow furrowed. *"How do we find peace in that?"*

"Consider it," Liana continued, feeling a flicker of warmth in their connection. *"Death is like a shadow that's always there but doesn't take away the light. It reminds us to live fully and cherish each moment."*

The group fell into contemplative silence, absorbing Liana's words. It felt as if they were holding hands in the darkness, each sharing their own fears and sorrows.

As the stars began to twinkle, Joseph broke the silence. *"I remember my father telling me stories of how he grew up as an orphan. He said family isn't just about blood; it's about the bonds we create."* His voice cracked, revealing the depths of his grief. Daisy's eyes glistened with tears. *"My parents always said that love is what makes a family. Even when those we love are gone, their essence remains in us."*

Omer looked at them all, a spark of hope igniting within him. *"So, we carry them with us. Their love shapes who we are and how we live."*

Liana nodded, feeling the warmth of their shared understanding. *"Rumi once wrote, 'Don't grieve. Anything you lose comes around in another form.' Our relationships may change, but their essence will always live on in us."*

As the night deepened, they shared laughter and memories, recalling quirks and stories that brought their loved ones to life in the midst of their grief. Liana spoke of her grandmother, recounting how she would weave tales that transcended time and space.

"Even now that she's gone, I can feel her presence guiding me," Liana said, her voice filled with love. *"It's as if she's a part of my journey, pushing me to embrace life."*

Daisy smiled softly. *"That's beautiful. It's like they never really leave us."*

"Exactly," Joseph agreed, wiping away a tear. *"Their love remains."*

As they gazed at the stars above, Liana felt a sense of peace washing over her. *"From death, there is one great lesson on love and connection. It teaches us to cherish the time we have with others and to allow ourselves to be vulnerable."*

Omer nodded thoughtfully. *"The fear of death often stems from our attachment to the physical. But love transcends that."*

In the following days, their discussions continued, weaving through philosophy and spirituality. They spent hours reflecting on the nature of life and death, each conversation drawing them closer.

One evening, while wandering through Istanbul's winding streets, they discovered a small art gallery filled with vibrant works. The paintings depicted the duality of life and death, intertwining flowers with skeletal figures, and dawns framed by shadows.

Liana was drawn to a particular piece—a tree with branches reaching upward and roots delving deep into the earth. *"This speaks to me,"* she whispered, captivated by its beauty.

"That piece represents the cycle of life," said an elderly artist nearby. *"We grow, we die, and nourish the earth for new life."*

Liana turned to him, her curiosity piqued. *"I've been exploring similar themes in my writing. I believe understanding death helps us appreciate life."*

"Indeed," the artist replied, nodding sagely. *"Many fear death, but it's part of our journey. Embracing it allows us to live more fully."*

As night fell, Liana left the gallery feeling invigorated. The conversation had blended with her reflections, inspiring her to channel her thoughts into her writing—a narrative that honored the beauty and tragedy of life.

That night, while bathed in moonlight, Liana wrote with fervor. *"Death teaches us to hold dear the present, to embrace those fleeting moments that give meaning to our days. Love is a force stronger than time, illuminating our paths even in the darkest of shadows."*

As she closed her journal, clarity washed over her. The philosophy of death wasn't an investigation into an end but an invitation to know life a little more deeply. It called upon them all to link with one another, embracing the journey regardless of the shadows that lay ahead.

Day by day, Liana found beauty in the mundane—the seconds of laughter with Joseph, the warmth of friendship with Omer and Daisy, and the quiet moments spent in her journal. All of these were gifts, woven into the complex tapestry of existence.

"To live is to love, to grieve, and to grow," Liana wrote as sleep reached for her like a soothing fog. *"And in the dance of shadows, we find the light."*

Chapter 17

The Depths of Desire

"In the depths of desire, where hearts intertwine and souls ignite, love becomes an eternal flame that whispers sweet secrets of forever."

The night was thick with anticipation, the air electric as Liana stood on her balcony, staring out at the sprawling city of Istanbul. The moon hung low, casting a silvery glow over the rooftops, and the shadows seemed to whisper secrets of forbidden desire. She could feel the weight of the world below her, yet all she could think about was Omer.

They had been dancing around their feelings for far too long, each stolen glance and lingering touch igniting a fire that threatened to consume them both. Liana's heart raced as she recalled the way Omer's eyes burned with intensity whenever they were near. The chemistry between them was undeniable, and the tension had reached a breaking point.

Later that night, a sudden knock on her door jolted her from her thoughts. She opened it to find Omer standing there, his silhouette framed by the dim light from the hallway. He looked rugged and wild, his hair tousled, and there was an urgency in his expression that sent shivers down her spine.

"I couldn't wait any longer," he said, stepping inside without invitation. The door clicked shut behind him, sealing them in a world of their own.

Liana's breath hitched as he closed the distance between them, his presence overwhelming. "What do you want, Omer?" she whispered, her voice trembling with a mixture of fear and longing.

He paused, searching her eyes as if looking for answers in the depths of her soul. "You know what I want," he replied, his voice low and husky, sending a thrill coursing through her. "I want you."

Before she could respond, he reached out and cupped her face in his hands, his touch igniting a fire beneath her skin. Liana's heart raced as he leaned in, his lips brushing against hers in a hesitant caress. The warmth of his breath mingled with hers, and time seemed to stand still in that fleeting moment.

Then, as if some unspoken agreement had been reached, he pressed his lips firmly against hers, deepening the kiss with a fervor that took her breath away. Liana melted against him, her body responding instinctively to the heat radiating from him. She had wanted this for so long, and now that it was happening, it felt like a dream.

His hands traveled to her waist, pulling her closer until there was no space left between them. She could feel his heart pounding in sync with her own, each beat echoing the intensity of their connection. The kiss grew more urgent, more demanding, as if they were both afraid of losing this moment.

Liana lost herself in him, her hands tangling in his hair as she pulled him deeper into the kiss. They stumbled back until they reached the wall, and she felt the cool surface against her back, contrasting with the heat of his body. Omer's hands roamed her curves, exploring the lines of her body as if she were a masterpiece he had longed to touch.

"Liana," he murmured against her lips, his voice thick with desire. "I've wanted you for so long."

"Then take me," she breathed, her voice laced with urgency. She wanted to drown in him, to surrender herself completely to the depths of their desire.

With a growl of determination, Omer lifted her effortlessly, pressing her against the wall. The world outside faded away as they became lost in each other, a tempest of longing and lust. Their kisses turned desperate, fueled by the pent-up tension of unspoken feelings.

As they broke apart for a moment, Liana met his gaze, her heart racing. "What if this changes everything?"

"Maybe it will," Omer replied, his expression serious yet filled with passion. "But I don't care. I want you now. Let's not think about tomorrow."

His lips crashed against hers again, and Liana surrendered to the moment, knowing they were stepping into a dangerous game. She wrapped her legs around his waist, urging him closer as he pressed his body against hers, their hearts pounding in a chaotic rhythm.

Time lost all meaning as they explored the depths of their desire, each kiss igniting a fire that threatened to consume them whole. Liana could feel the darkness surrounding them, but it only heightened her sense of thrill and urgency. They were caught in a whirlwind of passion, each movement sending shockwaves of pleasure through her body.

As the night wore on, the world outside ceased to exist. They were lost in each other, two souls intertwined in a dance of desire and lust, daring to explore the shadows that lingered between them. And in that moment, nothing else mattered but the intoxicating connection they shared, a connection that blurred the lines between love and obsession.

Liana knew that tomorrow would bring its own challenges and uncertainties, but for now, she was content to be enveloped in Omer's embrace, the weight of the world lifted as they surrendered to the darkness of their love.

The sun had barely risen over the horizon, painting the sky in hues of lavender and gold as Liana stirred awake, the memory of the previous night still tingling on her skin. She turned, half-expecting to see Omer beside her, but the space was empty. The warmth of his body lingered in her thoughts, a stark contrast to the cool morning air that enveloped her. It was as if the world outside was waking up to a new day while she still floated in the remnants of their passionate embrace.

The echoes of their whispered secrets and fervent kisses played in her mind like a sweet melody. They had crossed a threshold the night before, stepping into an uncharted territory filled with both exhilaration and uncertainty. She had never felt so alive, yet the lingering question of what lay ahead cast a shadow over her heart. As she rose from the bed, the sun filtered through her curtains, illuminating the small studio that had once felt like a sanctuary and now seemed to pulse with memories of Omer. Each brushstroke of their shared moments had painted the walls with a sense of longing and desire. She picked up her journal, flipping through the pages until she found her thoughts from the night before, the ink still fresh.

What does it mean to dream? Is it simply an escape, or is it a glimpse of our true selves?

She sighed, realizing that the dreamlike state she had entered with Omer was not just about passion but also about facing the truths hidden beneath their desires. In every dream, there was a thread of reality, and she couldn't ignore the weight of what they had begun.

Her thoughts were interrupted by a soft knock at the door. Heart racing, she opened it to find Omer standing there, a hesitant smile playing on his lips. He looked as if he had wrestled with his own thoughts throughout the night, the morning light catching the shadows beneath his eyes.

"Hey," he said, his voice low, a blend of tenderness and uncertainty.

"Hey," Liana replied, her pulse quickening at the sight of him. The air between them crackled with tension, a mixture of joy and fear. She stepped aside, allowing him to enter, and the moment he

crossed the threshold, it felt as if they were stepping back into that beautiful chaos they had created.

"I couldn't stop thinking about you," he confessed, running a hand through his hair, a nervous habit she had come to adore. *"About us."*

Liana's heart fluttered. *"Me too. But what does this mean? Last night was... incredible, but I don't want to complicate things between us."*

Omer took a step closer, his gaze intense and searching. *"I don't want to lose what we have, either. But I can't pretend that what happened was just a moment. It felt like something real, something we can't ignore."*

She nodded, feeling the weight of his words settle into her chest. *"I know. But there's so much at stake. Our friendship, the group... Everything feels different now."*

"Maybe different isn't a bad thing," he said, his voice firm yet soft. *"We're standing at the edge of something new, and I don't want to pull back. I want to explore this with you, whatever it may lead to."*

His honesty ignited something within her, a flicker of hope mingled with fear. *"But what if we cross that line and it all falls apart?"*

"Then we'll deal with it together," he replied, stepping even closer, his breath warm against her skin. The touch sent shivers through her, igniting the embers of desire that had never truly cooled. *"I want to know every part of you, Liana. I want to share my life with you, even the messy bits."*

She looked into his eyes, where the determination shimmered like the morning sun. *"I want that too,"* she admitted, her voice barely a whisper. *"But I need to know that we're in this together, no matter what happens."*

"Always," he said, reaching out to tuck a loose strand of hair behind her ear, his fingers lingering against her skin. The touch sent shivers through her, igniting the embers of desire that had never truly cooled.

As they pulled away, breathless, Liana knew they were at a precipice. The future lay before them, shrouded in uncertainty, but together, they could embrace the unknown. They would navigate the complexities of their relationship, weaving their friendship and romance into a tapestry rich with experience, desire, and vulnerability.

"Let's take this one step at a time," she said, her heart steadying.

Omer nodded, a smile breaking through the tension. *"One step at a time."*

With renewed determination, they stepped out onto the balcony, the city awakening beneath them. The sun rose higher, casting a golden glow that promised a new day—a day filled with possibilities, love, and the bittersweet taste of reality. Together, they were ready to embrace it all, standing on the threshold of their dreams, united by the passion that had ignited between them.

Chapter 18

Solace

"In the embrace of solace, we find the quiet strength to heal, the gentle light that guides us through our darkest moments."

The moon hung low in the sky, casting a silvery glow over Istanbul's rooftops, illuminating the cobblestone streets that had become familiar to Liana. Tonight, the air was thick with anticipation as she prepared for a gathering with her friends. The vibrant energy of the city pulsed around her, but her thoughts were consumed by one person—Omer.

Their connection had deepened over the past weeks, transforming into something she couldn't quite name but felt profoundly. In moments spent together, they had navigated shared laughter and lingering glances, each one drawing them closer, each touch igniting something within her that she had never fully acknowledged. As she adjusted her dress, she caught her reflection in the mirror, her heart racing at the thought of him.

"What is love if not a dance with shadows?" she murmured to herself, remembering Rumi's words that had always resonated with her. The notion of love being both light and darkness intrigued her, evoking a sense of longing intertwined with fear. Love was not just joy; it was vulnerability, the courage to embrace someone else's imperfections while revealing her own.

As she stepped into the bustling café where her friends gathered, Liana's pulse quickened. Omer sat at a corner table, his laughter mingling with the music playing in the background. His presence was magnetic, pulling her in like the tide. She took a moment to observe him, captivated by the way his eyes sparkled with mischief and kindness. A feeling of warmth spread through her; he had become the muse in her life's narrative.

"There you are!" Joseph called out, waving her over. She forced herself to look away from Omer, her heart fluttering as she approached the table.

"Hey!" Liana greeted, trying to mask her nervousness. Omer's gaze met hers, and a silent understanding passed between them.

It was as if the world had faded away, leaving just the two of them suspended in time.

"You look beautiful tonight," Omer said, a hint of sincerity in his voice. The compliment washed over her like a gentle wave, igniting a blush on her cheeks.

"Thanks! You look great too," she replied, her smile wide.

As the evening unfolded, the group engaged in lively conversations, sharing stories and laughter. But Liana's focus was drawn to Omer, the way he leaned in during discussions, the way his laughter felt like music. Each shared moment between them felt charged, like electricity crackling in the air.

"So, what's your take on love?" Joseph asked, turning to Liana, unaware of the tempest brewing in her heart.

"Love?" Liana echoed, her mind racing. *"I think it's... complicated. It's both beautiful and terrifying."* Her eyes flicked to Omer, who watched her intently, as if he were hanging onto every word.

"Complicated how?" Omer leaned forward, his curiosity evident.

"It's like..." Liana paused, searching for the right words, *"it's like navigating through shadows. There's light, but also fear and uncertainty."*

Omer nodded, his gaze never leaving hers. *"Rumi once said, 'The wound is the place where the Light enters you.' It's about embracing the pain, too."*

Her heart raced at his words, the wisdom within them resonating deeply. *"Exactly! We often fear the pain, but it's a part of the journey, isn't it?"*

"Yeah, it makes us who we are," he replied, his voice soft but firm.

As the night progressed, Liana found herself increasingly drawn to Omer, the air between them thick with unspoken feelings. They shared glances that lingered too long, laughter that held an undercurrent of something deeper.

At one point, their hands brushed against each other on the table, sending shivers down her spine. She felt a rush of warmth flood her cheeks, the moment stretching into eternity. The café, the noise, the laughter—everything faded, and it was just them, two souls dancing on the edge of something beautiful yet terrifying.

"Liana," Omer said suddenly, his voice low, pulling her from her thoughts. *"Can I ask you something?"*

Her heart raced as she nodded, intrigued and apprehensive.

"What do you want most in life?"

The question hung in the air, heavy with expectation. She searched his eyes, finding sincerity there. In that moment, the weight of the world shifted, and she felt an urge to bare her soul.

"I want to love deeply and be loved in return," she confessed, her voice steady yet vulnerable. *"But I also fear what that might mean. What if I lose myself in it? What if it hurts?"*

Omer's expression softened, understanding flooding his features. *"Love is a risk, Liana. But it's a beautiful risk. I think it's worth it."*

Her breath caught in her throat as his words settled in her heart. She felt a yearning to reach across the table, to close the distance, to entwine her fingers with his and never let go. But fear held her back, the shadows whispering doubts in her mind.

"What if I lose you?" she finally admitted, her voice barely above a whisper.

Omer leaned closer, his gaze unwavering. *"You won't lose me. We'll navigate it together, one step at a time."*

With those words, something shifted within Liana. She felt the weight of her fears begin to lift, replaced by the warmth of his conviction. She knew that love was not just about the light; it was about embracing the shadows as well, understanding that together they could illuminate the darkest corners of their hearts.

As the night wore on, Liana found herself dancing with the shadows of her thoughts, slowly unraveling the layers of her heart. Each laugh shared with Omer, each lingering touch, was a step closer to surrendering to the love that beckoned her.

"Rumi said, 'Let the beauty we love be what we do,'" she reflected, feeling the words wash over her. *"Maybe loving you is the most beautiful thing I could ever do."*

Omer smiled, his eyes alight with a mix of mischief and tenderness. *"Then let's embrace it, Liana. Let's dance in the light and the shadows, together."*

And in that moment, as they locked eyes, Liana knew she was ready to take that step. Love was waiting, a beautiful dance that promised both joy and vulnerability. She took a deep breath, allowing the possibilities to unfurl before her, knowing that together, they could navigate the intricate tapestry of their lives.

With her heart racing, she reached out, entwining her fingers with his, a silent promise woven between them. They were no longer just two friends caught in the current of life; they were partners in a dance, ready to explore the depths of their connection, where love flourished amidst both the light and the shadows.

Chapter 19

The Threshold of Dreams

"We stand as architects of our own destiny, where every whispered wish beckons the dawn of possibility."

As the golden rays of the sun spilled across Istanbul, Liana awoke with a renewed sense of purpose. She could feel the world pulsating with life outside her window, a vivid reminder of the stories waiting to be told. The previous night with Omer had opened her eyes to a new depth of feeling, and she longed to share her revelations—not just with her friends but with a wider audience—those who, like her, were navigating the tumultuous waters of young adulthood.

This chapter of her life felt crucial; she understood that each experience was a brushstroke on the canvas of her existence. Each laugh shared, each tear shed, was part of a greater tapestry, interwoven with the lives of those around her. With a spark of inspiration, she grabbed her journal, feeling the weight of her thoughts pressing against the pages, urging to be freed.

"Life is but a collection of moments," she began to write, *"each one a thread in the fabric of our being. We weave them together, creating a narrative that is uniquely ours."*

Liana's perspective on life had shifted, and she was determined to explore the intricate dance of youth—its joys, struggles, and the bittersweet nature of growing up. She envisioned a narrative that could resonate with young adults, a story that would capture the essence of their experiences while weaving in the philosophical undertones she had grown to cherish.

"Every young adult stands on the threshold of dreams," she penned, her thoughts flowing freely. *"We are explorers in a world that often feels vast and intimidating. Yet, within that uncertainty lies the beauty of possibility."*

That day, as she strolled through the bustling streets of Istanbul, Liana allowed her surroundings to fuel her creativity. She observed the diverse tapestry of life around her—vendors calling out, children playing, couples strolling hand in hand. Each moment felt like an invitation to delve deeper into the stories of those she passed.

Suddenly, her attention was drawn to a group of young people gathered in a park, their laughter ringing through the air. They were engaged in spirited discussions, debating everything from literature to philosophy. Curiosity piqued, Liana approached, intrigued by the vibrant energy surrounding them.

"What's the topic today?" she asked, a friendly smile on her face.

"We're discussing the concept of freedom," a tall girl with bright green hair replied, her eyes sparkling with enthusiasm. *"What does it mean to be truly free in today's world?"*

Liana felt a surge of excitement, eager to contribute to the conversation. *"I think freedom is about more than just physical liberation. It's about emotional and mental autonomy too. Many of us are trapped by societal expectations, our own fears, or the weight of our pasts."*

The group nodded in agreement, clearly appreciating her perspective. They welcomed her into their circle, and as the conversation flowed, Liana felt a sense of belonging that resonated deep within her. It reminded her of the importance of community in navigating the complexities of young adulthood.

As the sun began to set, painting the sky with brilliant shades of orange and purple, Liana found herself sharing her experiences—her journey through grief, the lessons she learned from loss, and her exploration of love and self-discovery.

"We are all navigating our own paths," she shared, *"and sometimes, it feels overwhelming. But those moments of struggle teach us resilience, shaping who we become."*

The discussion deepened, revealing the vulnerabilities that lay beneath the surface. Each individual shared their own battles: the pressure to succeed in their careers, the fear of disappointing loved ones, the struggle to maintain friendships amidst the chaos of life.

In that moment, Liana realized how crucial it was for young adults to connect, to voice their fears and dreams, and to support one another. The stories shared felt like tiny pieces of a greater narrative, each echoing the universal quest for identity and meaning.

"Isn't it ironic?" the green-haired girl mused, her expression contemplative. *"We yearn for connection, yet we often feel isolated in our struggles."*

Liana nodded, reflecting on the truth of her words. *"It's a paradox. We live in a world so interconnected, yet loneliness is prevalent. I think that's why storytelling is so powerful; it allows us to bridge those gaps, to find common ground."*

As the night wore on, the group shared their favorite quotes, books, and philosophies. Liana recalled Rumi's wisdom and the poetic essence of his words, recognizing how they resonated deeply with their discussions. She felt a profound sense of gratitude for the connections being forged, the authenticity of their shared experiences.

"The wound is the place where the Light enters you," Liana recited softly, her heart swelling with emotion. *"It reminds us that our struggles are not in vain; they shape us, guiding us toward our true selves."*

"Exactly!" someone chimed in, excitement crackling in the air. *"It's about embracing our scars and recognizing the strength they've given us."*

With the moon rising high, casting a gentle glow over the park, Liana realized that her experiences, her grief, her journey, were not solely her own; they were shared by countless others navigating the challenges of young adulthood. She understood that in her writing, she could encapsulate these shared struggles and triumphs, creating a narrative that would resonate far beyond her own life.

"Let's create something together," she proposed, her voice filled with enthusiasm. *"A collection of stories, reflections, and thoughts on what it means to be young today. We can explore love, loss, dreams, and the philosophies that guide us."*

The idea sparked excitement within the group. They began brainstorming, each contributing ideas, themes, and experiences they wanted to include. Liana felt invigorated, a sense of purpose coursing through her veins as they collaborated, weaving their individual narratives into a collective tapestry.

"This could be a platform for us to express ourselves," she said, her eyes shining with possibility. *"To share our journeys and show that we're not alone in this."*

As they discussed the project, Liana envisioned the impact their stories could have on others. They could inspire young adults who felt lost, offer solace to those grappling with similar struggles, and ignite a sense of hope amidst the chaos of life.

In the weeks that followed, the group met regularly, each session blossoming into vibrant discussions filled with laughter, tears, and shared vulnerabilities. They explored topics ranging from the weight of societal expectations to the beauty of personal freedom, creating a safe space where they could be authentically themselves.

Liana found herself writing more fervently than ever, her journal filling with ideas, snippets of dialogue, and philosophical musings. *"We are all threads in a grand tapestry,"* she wrote one night, *"woven together by our shared experiences, creating a beautiful narrative that is both unique and universal."*

The project became a sanctuary for Liana, a space where she could explore her thoughts on love, loss, and the complexities of growing up. Each story contributed was a brushstroke on the canvas of their shared experience, reflecting the myriad emotions and philosophies that defined their youth.

As their collective narrative began to take shape, Liana found herself reflecting on the profound connections they had forged. Each meeting felt like a step toward healing, a reminder that vulnerability was not a weakness but a strength that allowed them to transcend their individual struggles.

One night, as they gathered to review their progress, Liana felt a surge of gratitude for the journey they had embarked upon together. *"Thank you all for being so open and honest,"* she said, her voice trembling with emotion. *"This project has become so much more than I imagined. It's a testament to our resilience and the beauty of our shared humanity."*

The group nodded, the atmosphere charged with a sense of purpose and camaraderie. They were no longer just individuals navigating their paths; they had become a community, united in their quest for understanding and connection.

"Let's remember," Liana added, *"that our stories have the power to touch lives. We are not just writing for ourselves; we are creating a legacy that can resonate with others, inspire them to embrace their journeys."*

As they wrapped up the meeting, Liana felt a warmth spread through her heart. She had found her place in this world, surrounded by individuals who understood the intricacies of young adulthood, who embraced the struggles and celebrated the joys. Together, they were crafting a narrative that echoed the very essence of life—its beauty, its tragedy, and the profound connections that bind us all.

With the weight of their collective stories, Liana realized that she had discovered not just a community but a new sense of self. She was no longer just a wanderer in search of meaning; she was a storyteller, a bridge between experiences, weaving together the threads of life's rich tapestry.

"This is only the beginning," she whispered to herself as she walked home that night, the city alive with possibility. *"Together, we will illuminate the shadows and dance in the light."*

Chapter 20

Echoes of Longing

As dusk fell over Istanbul, Liana wandered through the cobbled streets, the city a living canvas painted in hues of orange and violet. The air was fragrant with spices, mingling with the soft sounds of evening and distant laughter. Yet, despite the vibrancy around her, her heart felt heavy with the weight of unspoken emotions. She found herself longing, not just for connection but for Omer—the warmth of his laughter, the depth of his gaze, and the electricity that sparked between them. Each step felt like a reminder of the tension coiling inside her. *"What if I lose him?"* she thought, grappling with the fear that held her back from fully embracing their love. The risk of losing what they had loomed large, casting shadows over her heart, but the ache of unfulfilled desire felt more suffocating.

"Love is a wild flame," she mused, her thoughts spiraling deeper into the complexity of her feelings. "It can either warm you or consume you whole." This truth resonated deeply within her, a reflection of her internal struggle as she stood at the crossroads of their passionate connection and the uncertainty of the future.

Liana sought refuge in her journal, its pages a sanctuary where she could explore her thoughts without judgment. She wrote furiously, pouring her heart out. *"Desire is a tempest within me, urging me to break free of the chains of fear."* Her pen moved with urgency, capturing the essence of her longing—a dance of ink and emotion that mirrored her internal turmoil. The act of writing became a cathartic release, as if each word freed her from the confines of her heart.

With every recollection of their moments together—the shared laughter, the brush of their hands, the way he lingered just a little too long in her gaze—her heart raced. They had forged a bond that was undeniable, yet something deeper lingered just beneath the surface, waiting to be explored. *"What if this longing is meant to be embraced?"* she questioned, the whisper of Rumi's wisdom echoing in her mind. *"You are not a drop in the ocean. You are the entire ocean in a drop."* The weight of this realization stirred something within her, reminding her of the vastness of her feelings and the possibilities that lay ahead.

Liana's resolve began to strengthen. She had spent too long locked in uncertainty, caught in the delicate web of their connection while the truth of her feelings simmered just beneath the surface. It was time to embrace the fullness of their love, to let go of any lingering doubts and allow herself to be vulnerable. *"If I do not take this leap, I risk losing the chance at something beautiful,"* she reflected, contemplating the weight of unexpressed feelings. The world around her felt vibrant, yet within her, a storm brewed, one that needed to be released.

Finding herself drawn to a quiet spot by the Bosphorus, Liana sat on a weathered bench, gazing at the shimmering water. The moonlight danced on the surface, casting a silvery glow that mirrored her heart's longing. In this moment of solitude, she allowed herself to envision the future she wanted with Omer—the life they could build together, filled with laughter, adventure, and unwavering support.

"What if we could create something extraordinary?" she pondered, hope igniting within her. The thought filled her with warmth, a flicker of excitement that enveloped her soul. "What if this love could transcend everything we've known?"

Liana closed her eyes, inhaling the night air deeply. The sweet scent of jasmine filled her lungs, grounding her as she explored the terrain of her emotions. *"Is love worth the risk?"* she whispered to the night, seeking answers among the stars that twinkled above. Rumi's words danced in her mind, reminding her of love's transformative power. *"Love is the bridge between you and everything."* She felt the truth of that statement resonate within her, a call to embrace the vulnerability that love demanded. To let go of the fear that bound her and to reach out toward Omer, to fully commit to their journey together.

As the evening deepened, Liana's thoughts crystallized. She recognized that the path to love was fraught with uncertainties, yet it was also rich with potential—potential for growth, for intimacy, for a shared journey that could transcend their existing relationship. The prospect of exploring what lay beneath the surface of their bond filled her with both excitement and trepidation. "I *can't continue to let fear dictate my choices,*" she resolved, a newfound determination rising within her. The echoes of her longing were not just whispers of desire; they were calls to action, urging her to step forward into the light of possibility.

With the moon shining brightly above, Liana felt a shift within her. The blend of hope and fear coalesced into something powerful— a promise to herself that she would embrace her feelings, whatever the outcome. The lingering questions were still there, but now they were accompanied by a flicker of courage. "*This is only the beginning,*" she told herself, heart racing with anticipation. As she rose from the bench, the city alive with possibility around her, Liana knew she was ready to embrace the fullness of her love for Omer, ready to explore the depths of what they had built together.

In the days that followed, the thrill of their love enveloped her, making every moment with Omer feel like a cherished treasure.

They shared meals at cozy cafes, wandered through bustling markets, and explored hidden gems of the city, each encounter deepening her appreciation for the bond they shared. Liana savored their time together, her heart swelling with affection as she witnessed Omer's joy and passion for life.

One evening, as they walked along the Galata Bridge, the sun setting behind them, Liana could feel the weight of the moment pressing down on her. The golden light illuminated Omer's face, highlighting the warmth in his eyes. She stole a glance at him, her heart racing, recognizing that they were on the brink of something profound.

"*Omer,*" she said softly, her voice a melody in the fading light. "*I want you to know how much you mean to me.*"

He turned to her, curiosity dancing in his gaze. "*You already know how I feel, Liana. But hearing you say that means everything.*"

A rush of gratitude filled her, and Liana took his hand, feeling the strength of their connection. "*I've never felt so alive, so free, as I do with you. I want to explore every facet of our love, to embrace all that we are together.*"

Omer's smile widened, his eyes sparkling with admiration. "*I understand how you feel. You inspire me to believe in a future full of dreams and endless possibilities.*"

As they stood together on the bridge, the beauty of Istanbul shimmering around them, Liana realized that they had crossed the threshold of their longing, stepping boldly into the embrace of love. Together, they watched the sun dip below the horizon, the vibrant colors reflecting the warmth in their hearts, symbolizing the promise of a new beginning.

And as the stars began to twinkle overhead, Liana knew she was exactly where she was meant to be—entangled in the threads of love that had woven their hearts together.

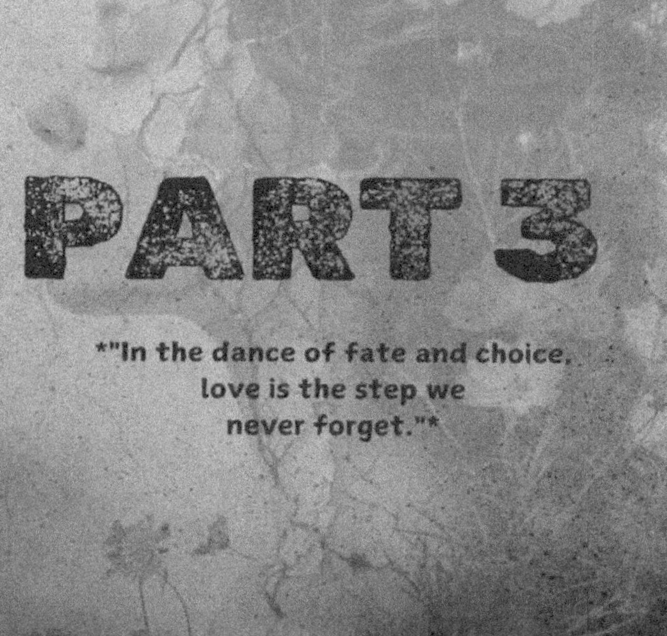

PART 3

*"In the dance of fate and choice,
love is the step we
never forget."*

Chapter 21

A Meeting with Rumi

The air was thick with the scent of blooming jasmine as Liana walked through the narrow, cobblestone streets of Istanbul. The sun dipped low on the horizon, casting a warm, golden hue over the city, bathing the ancient architecture in a soft glow. It was as if the universe conspired to create the perfect backdrop for an encounter she had been dreaming of—one with the great Rumi.

"In the stillness of the night, when the heart whispers its secrets, the soul finds its true voice," Liana recited from memory, her heart racing with anticipation. She had stumbled upon a quaint café tucked away in a secluded alley, its walls adorned with intricate calligraphy and art inspired by the revered Sufi poet. This was the place—a sanctuary of thought, a hub of spirituality.

Inside, the café was alive with murmurs of deep conversation and the soft strumming of a lute in the corner. Liana settled into a cozy nook, the atmosphere inviting her to lose herself in contemplation. As she sipped her tea, the rich aroma swirling around her, she felt a presence that transcended time.

Suddenly, the air shifted. Before her sat a figure dressed in flowing robes, his face radiating warmth and wisdom. His eyes sparkled with a depth of understanding that seemed to pierce through the veils of existence. "Welcome, Liana," he said, his voice resonating like a gentle melody. "You seek answers to questions that dwell in the hearts of many."

Liana's breath caught in her throat. *"Rumi? Is it really you?"*

"The essence of Rumi lives within us all," he replied, a smile dancing on his lips. *"I am but a reflection of the thoughts and feelings you carry. Speak, and let us explore the mysteries of life and death together."*

"I often find myself pondering the nature of existence," Liana began, her voice trembling with emotion. *"What is the purpose of life, and how does death fit into this intricate tapestry?"*

Rumi leaned back, his expression contemplative. *"Ah, my dear, life and death are but two sides of the same coin. One cannot exist without the other. Embrace each moment as a gift; every breath is a fleeting treasure."*

Liana felt a weight lift from her shoulders. *"But how do we confront the fear of death? It looms over us like a shadow, an inevitable conclusion to our journeys."*

"Fear is a construct of the mind," Rumi explained, his gaze piercing through the layers of her anxiety. *"When you realize that death is not an end, but a transformation, you will find peace. Just as the caterpillar becomes a butterfly, so too do our souls evolve beyond the physical realm."*

Liana considered his words, the truth resonating within her. *"But what of the grief we experience when we lose someone we love? How can we reconcile that pain?"*

"Grief is the echo of love," Rumi replied gently. *"It is a testament to the bonds we forge during our time together. In mourning, we honor the souls that have touched our lives. Instead of shying away from that pain, allow it to teach you about the depth of love."*

The warmth in Liana's heart grew, illuminating the shadows that had haunted her since her father's passing. *"So, you're saying that love and loss coexist, enriching our experiences?"*

"Indeed," Rumi said, leaning forward with intensity. *"Love transcends death. It is an energy that binds us, an eternal flame that cannot be extinguished. Your father lives on in your memories, your stories, and in the way you choose to love others."*

Liana felt tears welling up in her eyes, but this time, they were tears of gratitude. *"Thank you for your wisdom. It feels as though you've given me a gift—a new way of seeing the world."*

"The greatest gift is not what I offer, but what you discover within yourself," Rumi replied, his voice softening. *"Trust the journey. Seek beauty in every moment, even in the face of sorrow. Life is a dance, and each step, whether light or heavy, is a part of the divine choreography."* They sat in silence for a moment, the bustling café fading into the background as Liana absorbed his words. The weight of her past began to feel lighter, the burdens of grief transforming into a profound appreciation for the life she had shared with her father.

"What about dreams, Rumi? I often feel torn between my aspirations and the reality of my life," she confessed, her brow furrowing in contemplation.

"Dreams are the whispers of your soul," he replied, his eyes twinkling. *"They guide you toward your true purpose. Do not shy away from them; instead, let them illuminate your path. Each dream is a reflection of the divine within you, urging you to express your authenticity."*

A sense of clarity washed over Liana. The vision of her project—sharing the stories of her peers—began to crystallize in her mind. "So, *if I pursue my dreams, I'm honoring the essence of who I am?*"

"Yes, *precisely!*" Rumi exclaimed, his passion igniting. "*Your dreams are a manifestation of your spirit's desires. The world needs your voice, your story. Do not hesitate to share it, for in doing so, you inspire others to embrace their journeys.*"

Liana's heart soared at the thought. "*Thank you, Rumi. I feel as if I've been given permission to live fully, to embrace the journey, however messy it may be.*"

"*The path is never linear,*" Rumi said, his tone gentle yet firm. "Embrace *the twists and turns, the challenges and triumphs. Each experience adds color to your canvas. Remember, it is in the struggle that you find your strength.*"

"*Yet, in love, there's also pain,*" Liana added, her thoughts drifting to Omer. "*Why must love be intertwined with sorrow? It feels like a double-edged sword.*"

Rumi nodded thoughtfully. "*Ah, my dear, love is a deep well, filled with both joy and sorrow. It is in that depth where we discover the essence of our humanity. As I once* wrote: '*The wound is the place where the Light enters you.' Embrace the pain, for it is a testament to your capacity to love.*"

Liana pondered his words, a mix of longing and heartache swirling within her. "So, you're saying that through love, we encounter our vulnerabilities, but also our strengths?"

"Exactly," Rumi affirmed, a glimmer of understanding in his eyes. "In love, we are laid bare, revealing our most authentic selves. The joy of connection brings light, while the sorrow of loss teaches resilience. *When the soul lies down in that grass, the world is too full to talk about ideas, language, even the phrase each other— doesn't make any sense.*' In love, we find unity, even amidst the pain."

Liana felt a spark ignite within her. "And perhaps that unity extends beyond our relationships with others to the love we cultivate for ourselves?"

"Ah, self-love is the foundation upon which all other love is built," Rumi replied, his voice rich with insight. "*'Love yourself completely, and you will find the universe responding in kind.*' When you nurture your spirit, you become a vessel for love to flow freely, allowing you to connect deeply with those around you."

The conversation flowed like a river, each word deepening Liana's understanding of life's complexities. "And what of the fear that accompanies love?" she asked, her heart still wrestling with uncertainty. "How do we protect ourselves while allowing ourselves to be vulnerable?"

"Love is inherently risky, yet it is also the most rewarding journey one can undertake," Rumi mused. *"Why are you so busy with this or that or good or bad; pay attention to how things blend.'* When you embrace love, you also embrace the unknown. Trust that your heart knows the way, and let go of the need for control."*

Liana felt a rush of warmth envelop her. *"So, it's about surrendering to the process?"*

"Precisely," Rumi smiled. *"Surrender is not defeat; it is an act of courage. In surrendering, you allow love to unfold naturally, without the constraints of fear or expectation. This is where true magic resides."*

As their time together drew to a close, Liana felt an overwhelming sense of gratitude. *"Will I ever see you again?"* she asked, a hint of longing in her voice.

"You will find me in the words you write, in the stories you tell," Rumi replied, his presence shimmering like a dream. *"Whenever you seek me, look within. I am never far away."*

With that, he rose, the atmosphere shimmering with his energy. As he turned to leave, Liana felt an unshakable sense of purpose settling within her.

"Thank you, Rumi," she whispered, her heart full. *"For everything."*

The moment he disappeared from view, Liana felt the weight of the world shift on its axis. The café's lively sounds returned, but she saw everything with new eyes. The laughter, the conversations, the stories unfolding around her—it all felt interconnected, a tapestry of life that she was now a part of.

With a renewed sense of clarity and determination, she pulled out her journal, ready to capture the essence of their conversation. The words flowed freely as she wrote about life, death, love, and the beauty of existence. "*Life is a journey filled with colors, pain, and joy,*" she scribbled. "Each moment is a brushstroke, creating a masterpiece unique to each soul."

As the evening waned, Liana realized that she was not just a seeker of truth; she was now a storyteller — a weaver of narratives that could inspire and connect. She would carry Rumi's wisdom with her, and in sharing her journey, she would honor the essence of life itself.

"*I will illuminate the shadows,*" she vowed, her heart alight with purpose. "I *will share my voice and the voices of those around me. Together, we will weave a story that echoes through the ages.*"

With the moon rising high, Liana left the café, stepping into the vibrant Istanbul night, ready to embrace whatever the journey ahead had in store. The whispers of Rumi lingered in her heart, guiding her steps as she ventured into the realm of dreams, life, and the profound connection that bound them all.

As she walked through the city's enchanting streets, Liana reflected on the love she felt for Omer, a love filled with promise yet shadowed by uncertainty. *"What is love,"* she pondered, *"if not a dance of joy and heartache?"* Each memory of their moments together brought both warmth and a pang of longing.

In her mind, she echoed Rumi's words: *"Love is the bridge between you and everything."* It was a bridge she wanted to cross, yet doubt lingered like a fog.

But as Rumi had taught her, love was not just a feeling; it was a journey. With each step, Liana felt the weight of her fears lift, replaced by a surge of courage. She envisioned herself sharing her stories, not just to heal herself but to illuminate the paths of others who walked similar journeys.

"Just as Rumi believed, I can find beauty in my scars," she thought. "I will turn my pain into poetry, weaving it into the tapestry of life."

With newfound resolve, Liana found herself at the waterfront, the Bosphorus shimmering under the moonlight. The waters whispered secrets of ages past, of love stories that echoed through time. She could almost hear Rumi's voice in the gentle lapping of the waves, urging her to embrace her own narrative.

"Let yourself be silently drawn by the strange pull of what you really love. It will not lead you astray," she recalled, her heart swelling with inspiration.

Liana closed her eyes, letting the cool breeze envelop her, feeling connected to the essence of the universe. It was a moment of clarity—a realization that love, in all its forms, was worth pursuing. Whether it was her love for Omer, her passion for storytelling, or the connection to her lost father, each thread was vital to her existence.

As the night deepened, Liana whispered a silent promise to herself and the universe: "I will not shy away from love. I will embrace it fully, with all its complexities. I will tell my story and honor the stories of those around me."

With the moon as her witness, Liana stepped forward, ready to face the myriad of emotions life would throw her way, armed with Rumi's timeless wisdom and a heart wide open to love. The journey ahead was uncertain, but for the first time in a long while, she felt ready to welcome it all.

She pulled out her diary, words fusing in her mind when she began to write:

In the garden of love, where the heart takes flight,
Every bloom is a promise, every star is light.
Oh, the dance of the soul in the quiet of night,
In shadows and whispers, we find our delight.

Life is a river, winding through the land,
Each twist a discovery, each turn a hand.

With joy and with sorrow, we learn to expand,
Embracing the journey, a divine, sacred strand.

Peace is the silence that lingers within,
A gentle reminder where all dreams begin.
In the stillness of being, we find what has been,
The echoes of love, in the spaces between.

Death is not darkness; it's a doorway, my friend,
A passage to realms where the soul will ascend.
With each end, a new start, where journeys blend,
In the heart's endless cycle, we learn to transcend.

So let love be your compass, let it guide your way,
In the tapestry woven, it's the light of your day.
For we are but vessels in this fleeting display,
In Rumi's sweet whispers, we find our ballet.

Chapter 22

The Awakening

The soft morning sunlight seeped through Liana's window, creating a cozy illumination in her room. She woke up feeling clear and driven in a way that was both unfamiliar and exciting. The reverberations of her encounter with Rumi resonated in her thoughts, giving her soul a fresh resolve. The possibilities outside her window were abundant, and she was prepared to welcome them.

"Life is a river," she whispered to herself, recalling Rumi's words. *"It flows, twists, and turns, carrying us to places we never imagined."* While getting ready for the day, she felt a strong desire to communicate her thoughts and release her emotions in her journal. Every time she made a mark with the pen, it was like a

form of meditation, commemorating how far she had come on her journey.

"Yesterday, I found myself in the presence of pure wisdom," she penned, feeling her heart beat with excitement. *"Rumi pointed out to me that life is not a straight line but a holy dance, an expedition full of love and sorrow, joy and sadness."* She pondered on the life-changing event as the ink spilled without hesitation.

Liana chose to stroll alongside the Bosphorus, with the glistening waters reflecting the sunny sky. With every step she took, she noticed the burden of her history diminishing, as a rejuvenating feeling of optimism took its place. The city pulsed with vitality, teeming with energy, as she sensed her heartbeat aligning with Istanbul's.

While she roamed, she thought about her friends Daisy, Omer, and Joseph, all of whom had been important in her adventure. She wanted to pass on the knowledge she gained and motivate others, just as Rumi had motivated her.

She discovered a peaceful location by the water where she could sit and ponder. The soothing symphony of waves lapping against the shore filled the air, accompanying her thoughts. *"How can I pass on this brightness to others?"* she quietly contemplated, speaking in a faint voice.

All of a sudden, she noticed Omer approaching her, his face adorned with a relaxed smile. *"Liana! Keep up the good work! Here you are. I have been searching for you."*

She told him she needed time to ponder, gesturing for him to take a seat next to her. *"I had an amazing time."*

Omer became curious as he sat down beside her. *"Spill all the details to me. You appear changed—brighter."*

"I met Rumi," she started, feeling a rush of excitement. While she told her story, Omer paid close attention, his facial expressions changing from doubt to interest. *"He discussed life, death, love, and the significance of dreams. It felt like he delved into my innermost being and sparked a fire within me."*

"Have you heard of Rumi? Do you mean Rumi?" Omer's eyes grew wider. *"Wow, that is amazing! What was his statement?"*

Liana explained, with a voice full of emotion, that he said our dreams are the whispers of our souls. *"He prompted me to accept the journey, regardless of its twists and turns. This is all a part of the rhythm of life."*

Omer nodded, taking in what she said. *"It appears deeply meaningful. What do you plan to do next?"*

She declared her desire to share her journey, as well as their journeys, with others, feeling a surge of passion. *"I aim to preserve our narratives and establish a space for bonding, to reassure individuals that they have companionship."*

Omer's enthusiasm shone brightly on his face. *"Wow, that idea is fantastic! We might consider launching a blog or organizing events. We can ask others to tell us about their experiences, their aspirations, and their obstacles."*

"Precisely!" Liana responded, feeling her heart pound with excitement. *"I aim to establish a community—a place where we can unite, receive assistance, and rejoice in the wonders of life."*

As they talked, Liana felt a sense of unity growing between them. The idea of collaborating with her friends, weaving their stories into a tapestry of shared experiences, filled her with exhilaration.

Days turned into weeks, and Liana, Omer, Daisy, and Joseph came together to brainstorm ideas for their project. They met in cafés, parks, and their homes, brainstorming names, themes, and goals. Liana's journal became a hub of creativity as they mapped out their vision.

They decided to call their project *"Whispers of the Heart,"* a tribute to the conversations and connections that Rumi had inspired. Their goal was to create a platform for storytelling, where individuals could share their experiences, vulnerabilities, and wisdom.

Liana's heart swelled with excitement as they worked together, laughter and deep conversations filling the air. With each passing day, she felt a sense of purpose solidifying within her. She was no longer just a seeker of truth; she was a vessel for others' stories, a bridge connecting lives through shared experiences.

One evening, as they gathered in Liana's living room, she felt a surge of gratitude. *"I can't believe how far we've come in such a short time,"* she said, looking around at her friends. *"This is just the beginning. I feel as if we're creating something magical."*

Daisy, ever the dreamer, chimed in, *"It's like we're weaving a tapestry of voices, each thread representing a different journey. Together, we'll create something beautiful."*

"Exactly!" Liana exclaimed. *"We all have our struggles and triumphs. By sharing them, we can help others feel seen and understood."*

Joseph nodded in agreement. *"And it's important to remind people that they're not alone in their experiences. We're all navigating this intricate dance of life together."*

As their project blossomed, they decided to host their first gathering—a storytelling evening in a cozy café. Liana felt a rush of excitement and nervousness as they planned the details. They spread the word through social media, inviting friends, family, and even strangers to come and share their stories.

On the day of the event, the café was filled with an eclectic mix of people, all drawn together by the promise of connection and understanding. Liana stood at the front, her heart racing as she welcomed everyone. *"Thank you for being here. Tonight is about sharing our journeys—our whispers of the heart. Every story matters, and together we create a beautiful tapestry of life."*

As the evening unfolded, individuals began to share their stories—tales of love, loss, dreams, and resilience. Liana listened intently, her heart swelling with compassion and understanding. Each voice resonated within her, reinforcing the belief that they were all connected in their humanity.

As the night drew to a close, Liana felt a profound sense of fulfillment. Rumi's wisdom echoed in her mind—*"The wound is the place where the Light enters you."* She realized that by embracing their wounds and sharing their stories, they had created a safe space for healing and connection.

After the event, Liana, Omer, Daisy, and Joseph gathered together, their hearts alight with excitement. *"This was incredible!"* Liana said, her eyes sparkling. *"I feel like we've touched lives tonight."*

"Absolutely," Omer replied, his voice filled with awe. *"I think we've started something beautiful."*

"And it's only the beginning," Daisy added, a smile brightening her face. *"Imagine where this journey could take us."*

Liana felt a surge of gratitude for the friendships that had blossomed during this journey. She realized that meeting Rumi had not only changed her life but had also set in motion a series of events that would ripple through the lives of others.

"Thank you all for being part of this," Liana said, her voice thick with emotion. *"Together, we're creating a community that celebrates life in all its complexities."*

As they stood together, united by a shared purpose, Liana felt a deep sense of belonging. The journey ahead was uncertain, but she knew they would face it together, guided by the light of their shared stories and the wisdom of Rumi that had ignited their spirits.

And in that moment, she understood that life was not just a solitary path; it was a beautiful dance of connections, woven together by the whispers of the heart.

After their initial storytelling event went well, Liana experienced a range of emotions as she adjusted to her new journey in the weeks that followed. The first excitement of linking had grown into a deep comprehension of the delicacy and loveliness of life. However, when the sun went down, shadows tended to grow longer, and Liana started to face challenges that came from within her own thoughts.

On a grey morning, Liana sat at her desk with her journal open, but she couldn't find the right words. While the café was bustling with activity, she was surrounded by a disquieting stillness. She pondered, with her pen suspended above the paper, *"What if everything is just a trick of the mind? What if I fall short?"* The uncertainties sneaked in like unwanted visitors, murmuring doubts that choked her soul.

She remembered when Rumi said, *"The wound is where the Light enters you,"* but today, even that insight seemed far away. She had to face the brewing storm of emotions inside her, the tumultuous sea that was putting her confidence at risk.

Later that day, Liana chose to go to the tiny library hidden in a peaceful part of the city. It served as her refuge, a space where she could disappear amidst the bookcases, engulfed by the ideas of numerous individuals who had faced their own challenges. While walking among the aisles, she ran her fingers over the book spines, sensing the heavy burden of her hardships.

She discovered a well-read copy of *"The Essential Rumi"* and took it off the bookcase. She opened it randomly and recited to herself: *"The beauty of the heart is the only beauty that endures."* The words struck a profound chord within her, reverberating the principles she cherished. Still, she couldn't shake the question: *How could she fully accept?*

While settling into a peaceful nook at the library, Liana pondered the obstacles ahead of her. She reflected on the core of encountering challenges. She remembered a valuable teaching from her time with Rumi: impediments serve as mentors, leading towards self-realization.

She thought that sinking into despair was simple, but real progress arose from finding one's way through the darkness. Liana breathed in deeply, sensing the air, giving her lungs a sense of purpose. *"What if I viewed my obstacles as opportunities for personal development?"*

Motivated, she started jotting down in her diary, turning her sense of inadequacy into a story of strength. She wrote that each challenge is a stepping stone. *We discover our strength when we confront our fears.* She let the ink flow without restriction as she penned her thoughts, forming a philosophy that combined her own experiences with the knowledge of those who came before her.

As she wrote, she reflected on the many individuals she had met through *"Whispers of the Heart."* Each story shared illuminated the diverse paths of struggle and triumph. *"Perhaps,"* she pondered, *"my own challenges can serve as a thread in the tapestry of connection."*

Later that week, Liana faced her first significant challenge in the new project. One of the key members of their team, Joseph, had expressed doubts about their direction. He was concerned that they were losing focus, drifting away from their original mission. This confrontation caught Liana off guard, stirring up a whirlwind of emotions within her.

"Liana, I believe in what we're doing, but I think we need to reevaluate," Joseph had said, his voice steady but filled with concern. *"We've lost some of the rawness that drew people in."*

"What do you mean?" Liana asked, feeling defensive. The air felt thick with unspoken tensions as she absorbed his words. *"I thought we were on the right track."*

"We are, but we also need to remain true to ourselves," he replied, his gaze unwavering. *"I think we need to dig deeper into our stories and allow our vulnerabilities to shine through."*

Liana felt her heart race. His words struck a chord deep within her. *"You're right,"* she admitted, her voice softening. *"I've been so focused on the idea of success that I may have overlooked the essence of our journey."*

That evening, she sat on her balcony, watching the sunset paint the sky in hues of gold and crimson. The beauty of the moment contrasted sharply with her inner turmoil. As the sun dipped below the horizon, she recalled a lesson from her meeting with Rumi: *"The wound is the place where the Light enters you."* She understood now that vulnerability was not a weakness; it was a strength.

"I need to embrace my own wounds," she whispered to herself. *"Only then can I encourage others to do the same."* In that moment, she felt a flicker of hope ignite within her—a reminder that challenges could transform into opportunities for connection and healing.

The following week, Liana called for a team meeting. She wanted to address the concerns Joseph had raised and encourage everyone to share their thoughts openly. *"I've been reflecting on our journey,"* she began, her voice steady yet filled with emotion. *"I realize that while we've accomplished so much, we must also remain true to the heart of our mission."*

"It's important that we share our true selves," she continued, *"to be vulnerable and honest about our struggles. That's where the real connection lies."*

Daisy nodded, her eyes bright with understanding. *"I think we've all been holding back,"* she admitted. *"We need to allow our stories to reflect our challenges, not just our successes."*

As they discussed their ideas, Liana felt a renewed sense of purpose. They decided to create a series of storytelling evenings dedicated to vulnerability, inviting participants to share their most challenging experiences. *"We want to create a space where people can feel safe to express their fears and doubts,"* Liana said, her heart swelling with conviction.

As the event approached, Liana felt a mix of excitement and anxiety. Would people be willing to share their struggles? Would they resonate with the theme of vulnerability? The doubts crept in again, but this time, she confronted them with Rumi's wisdom: *"Don't grieve. Anything you lose comes round in another form."*

On the night of the event, the café buzzed with anticipation. Liana stood at the front, her heart racing. She felt the energy of the room—a mixture of nervousness and excitement. *"Welcome, everyone,"* she began, her voice steady. *"Tonight, we're here to embrace our vulnerabilities and share our stories of struggle."*

As the evening unfolded, one by one, individuals stepped forward to share their experiences. Liana listened, her heart breaking and healing with each story. There was a young woman who had battled anxiety, an older man who had lost a child, and a couple who had faced the collapse of their dreams. Each voice resonated deeply, reminding Liana of the strength found in shared humanity.

When Liana finally took the stage, she felt a mix of vulnerability and empowerment. *"I want to share something personal,"* she began. *"I've struggled with feelings of inadequacy and doubt. Meeting Rumi changed my perspective, but I still face challenges every day. I realized that it's okay to not have it all figured out."*

"Embracing our wounds," she continued, *"allows us to connect with others on a deeper level. It's in our struggles that we find the light to illuminate the paths of those around us."* As she spoke, she felt the weight of her insecurities lifting, replaced by a sense of solidarity with the audience.

The night ended in tears and laughter, a beautiful reminder of the power of vulnerability. Liana felt a profound connection with those who had shared their stories, realizing that together, they were creating a safe space for healing and growth.

In the days that followed, Liana continued to face challenges, but she approached them with a new mindset. *"Every challenge is an opportunity for growth,"* she reminded herself. With each struggle, she felt her resolve strengthen, her understanding of life deepening.

And as Rumi had once said, *"The wound is the place where the Light enters you."* Liana understood that it was through her challenges that she would continue to find her voice, illuminating the path not only for herself but for others navigating their own storms.

In embracing her struggles, she discovered a profound truth: the journey was not about avoiding the darkness but dancing with it, allowing the light to shine through the cracks, creating a tapestry of resilience, hope, and connection.

Chapter 23

Tying the Knot

"To tie the knot is to weave two lives into a single tapestry, where every thread of love, hope, and promise binds them closer, creating a masterpiece that endures the test of time."

The air was electric with excitement as Liana prepared for the evening she had been dreaming about. After weeks of reflection and growth, she felt a renewed sense of purpose, especially when it came to her relationship with Omer. Their bond had deepened significantly, forged in the fires of vulnerability and shared experiences. The storytelling events had not only allowed her to connect with others but had also solidified her feelings for him.

It was a warm evening, and the café where they had first met buzzed with chatter and laughter. Liana had decided to turn this familiar setting into the backdrop for a moment that would change their lives forever. She had chosen a secluded corner table, adorned with soft candlelight and fresh flowers, creating an intimate atmosphere that echoed their shared love story.

As Liana set the table, her heart raced with anticipation. She had always believed in the magic of moments like these, where everything aligned to create something unforgettable. Omer would arrive any minute, and she wanted this evening to be perfect.

When Omer walked through the door, his eyes lit up at the sight of her. He approached with a warm smile, his presence filling the space with an undeniable warmth. *"What's all this?"* he asked, taking in the beautiful setup.

"Just a little surprise," Liana replied, her heart fluttering. She gestured for him to sit. *"I wanted to create a special moment for us."*

As they settled in, Liana felt the weight of the proposal resting heavily in her heart. The air was thick with unspoken words, but tonight was not about uncertainty; it was about commitment.

"You know," she began, her voice steady but filled with emotion, *"the past few months have changed me. I've learned so much about*

myself, about love, and about the importance of sharing our journeys."

Omer nodded, his gaze focused on her. *"You've always had a way of finding light in the darkest moments. It's one of the things I admire most about you."*

Liana felt a rush of warmth at his words. *"But it's not just me. It's been us, Omer. You've been my anchor through everything."*

They shared a moment of silence, the connection between them deepening. Liana could feel the emotions swirling inside her, a mix of excitement and nervousness. This was the moment she had been waiting for, the culmination of their love story.

"I've been thinking a lot about our future," she continued, her voice gaining strength. *"About what it means to be truly committed to one another."*

Omer leaned forward, his expression serious. *"I want to build a future with you, Liana. I can't imagine my life without you."*

Her heart soared at his words. This was the opening she had been hoping for. With a deep breath, she reached into her bag and pulled out a small velvet box. *"Omer,"* she said, her voice steady, *"I've been thinking about how to express my love for you in a way that reflects what we've built together."*

His eyes widened in surprise as she opened the box, revealing a simple but elegant ring, adorned with a small gemstone that caught the candlelight. *"I want to take this journey with you,"* she said, her heart pounding. *"Will you marry me?"*

The moment hung in the air, suspended between anticipation and reality. Omer's expression shifted from surprise to sheer joy. *"Liana,"* he breathed, *"are you serious?"*

"I am," she replied, her voice filled with conviction. *"I've never been more certain of anything in my life. You are my partner, my best friend, and I want to spend the rest of my life with you."*

Tears glistened in his eyes as he took the ring from the box, gently slipping it onto her finger. *"Yes, a thousand times yes!"* he exclaimed, his voice choked with emotion. *"I can't believe you did this. You make me so incredibly happy."*

They embraced, their hearts beating in sync as they held each other tightly. Liana could feel the warmth of love enveloping them, the challenges of the past melting away in the face of their shared commitment.

As they pulled back, Omer cupped her face in his hands, his eyes searching hers. *"We'll navigate everything together, won't we? No matter what life throws at us?"*

"Always," she promised, feeling a wave of certainty wash over her. *"We'll face everything together, just like we always have."*

They spent the rest of the evening reveling in their love, talking about their dreams for the future and the life they would build together. The café, once just a backdrop to their beginnings, transformed into a place of promise and joy, echoing with laughter and whispers of love.

As the night drew to a close, Liana felt a profound sense of peace. She had finally tied the knot with Omer—not just with a ring but with a promise of love, understanding, and commitment. Their journey was just beginning, and she was ready to embrace every moment of it, hand in hand with the man she loved.

"A thousand times yes." That was how Liana had responded when she finally found the courage to propose to Omer. Now, their lives were filled with the buzz of wedding preparations, excitement hanging in the air like the scent of blooming flowers. As the days turned into weeks, Liana and Omer transformed their dreams into reality, each moment a step closer to their beautiful celebration of love.

Daisy and Joseph, their closest friends, were swept up in the whirlwind of planning. They were bursting with excitement and, in their eagerness, had become an unstoppable duo, ready to take on the world—or at least, the wedding preparations.

Liana chuckled to herself as she watched them. Daisy was animatedly flipping through a stack of wedding magazines, her dark curls bouncing as she pointed out various ideas, while Joseph rolled his eyes but couldn't hide his grin. They had both been excited from the very beginning, but now, with the wedding just weeks away, their energy had reached a new level.

"Liana! Look at this dress!" Daisy exclaimed, holding up a glossy magazine page that showcased a stunning gown embellished with delicate lace and intricate beadwork. "You should totally try something like this! It's perfect for you!"

Liana smiled, knowing that Daisy was always the one to bring out the best in her. "I love it, but I think I want something a little simpler, maybe more in tune with the Istanbul vibe."

"Simple is overrated!" Joseph chimed in, his tone teasing. "It's your wedding! You should shine brighter than the sun!"

"And I'll probably be more like a nervous sunflower," Liana joked, shaking her head as she glanced around the room filled with fabric swatches and decorations they had collected. "But I appreciate the vote of confidence."

The four of them had decided to make the planning process a group effort, each contributing their unique perspectives. Liana focused on the overall vision, while Omer helped with the logistics, bringing his practicality to the table. Meanwhile, Daisy and Joseph were on a mission, bouncing from store to store, gathering ideas and supplies, and ensuring that everything would be perfect for the big day.

One afternoon, they all gathered in Liana's apartment, which had transformed into a makeshift planning headquarters. Swatches of fabric hung from every corner, and the aroma of freshly brewed coffee wafted through the air, mingling with the laughter and chatter.

"So, what's next on our list?" Omer asked, leaning back in his chair, a content smile on his face as he watched his friends in action.

"We need to finalize the colors!" Daisy said, her eyes sparkling with enthusiasm. She began laying out a series of vibrant colors on the table: deep turquoise, warm gold, and soft blush pink. "I think these would look stunning together, don't you?"

Liana's heart warmed at the sight of her friends' enthusiasm. "They are beautiful! I love how they represent the vibrant spirit of Istanbul."

Joseph clapped his hands together, his excitement palpable. "Perfect! Let's get swatches for the table settings and maybe some flowers that match. We need to make this a feast for the eyes!"

The energy in the room was electric. They spent hours discussing every detail, from the decorations to the menu, laughing as they stumbled over ideas and plans. They even created a group chat dedicated to the wedding, where Daisy and Joseph would send memes and inspiration, keeping the excitement alive between planning sessions.

"Can we just take a moment to appreciate how incredible this is?" Joseph said one day, his tone sincere. "We're planning a wedding in Istanbul! How many people can say that?"

"Not many," Liana agreed, her heart swelling with gratitude. "I feel so lucky to have you both by my side."

As the days turned into weeks, the wedding preparations took on a life of their own. They visited local markets in search of unique items to add a personal touch to the celebration. One day, they found themselves wandering through the Grand Bazaar, the air thick with the scent of spices and the vibrant sounds of merchants calling out to customers. Liana felt as if they were stepping into a treasure trove.

"Look at these lanterns!" Daisy exclaimed, picking up a beautifully crafted lamp adorned with intricate patterns. "They'd make the perfect centerpiece!"

Liana felt her spirit lift at the sight of the lanterns, their colors echoing the hues they had chosen. "They're gorgeous! Let's get a few and see how they look together."

As they explored, Joseph couldn't resist the temptation to haggle. His playful banter with the shopkeepers filled the market with laughter, and Liana couldn't help but admire how he brought lightness to every situation. Daisy and Liana exchanged amused glances, their hearts full as they watched their friend charm the locals.

With each visit to a market or store, the bond between the four of them deepened. They became more than friends; they became family, sharing stories, dreams, and the kind of laughter that echoed long after the moment had passed.

As the wedding day approached, Liana found herself lost in thought one evening, surrounded by the remnants of their planning chaos. She sat on her balcony, looking out at the city that had embraced her. The lights twinkled like stars, and the sound of the street below felt like a comforting lullaby. Omer joined her, wrapping his arms around her waist, grounding her in the moment.

"What are you thinking about?" he asked softly.

"How incredible this journey has been," she replied, leaning into him. "I can't believe how much we've done together."

"And it's just the beginning," Omer said, his voice steady. "We have so many adventures ahead."

Liana felt a rush of love for him, knowing that they would face whatever came next together. As she looked into his eyes, she saw the promise of a future filled with warmth, laughter, and a love that felt like home.

"Thank you for being my partner in all of this," she said, her voice barely above a whisper.

"Always," he replied, pressing a kiss to her forehead.

With the support of their friends and the excitement of their wedding day approaching, Liana felt a renewed sense of hope. The journey they had taken together, marked by laughter, friendship, and love, was just the beginning of the story they would write together. The wedding would be a celebration not just of their love but of the incredible bond they shared with those who meant the most to them.

In the heart of Istanbul, amid the bustling markets and vibrant culture, Liana and Omer were crafting a celebration that reflected not only their love but the lives they had intertwined with others. The anticipation swelled within her, filling her with a sense of joy that was infectious.

The day would soon come when they would step into the next chapter of their lives, hand in hand, surrounded by those they cherished most. The preparations were merely a prelude to the beautiful symphony of love that awaited them, a melody composed of laughter, friendship, and an occasional bout of chaos that seemed to follow them wherever they went.

As the countdown to the wedding dwindled, Liana and Omer found themselves knee-deep in the whirlwind of planning. One evening, they gathered at Liana's apartment, which had transformed into a creative war room, complete with colorful swatches, wedding magazines strewn about like confetti, and an unending supply of snacks.

"So, what's next on the agenda?" Omer asked, trying to sound serious, but the mischievous grin on his face suggested he was secretly hoping for some fun.

"We need to finalize the seating chart," Liana replied, rolling her eyes playfully. "Or, as I like to call it, the game of musical chairs, where no one gets a seat, and everyone is mildly offended."
Joseph burst out laughing, "It's like Tetris, but with family drama!"

Daisy chimed in, "You know what? We should assign an official 'Peacekeeper' to each table. I volunteer as tribute!" She raised her hand dramatically, pretending to wield a sword. "I promise to mediate any disputes over who gets the last piece of cake!"

"I can already see the headlines: 'Wedding Ends in Cake War: Friends Emerge Covered in Frosting,'" Joseph quipped, leaning back in his chair, hands behind his head. "Perfect for the wedding album!"

Liana laughed, "Maybe we should just keep it simple. Let's sit the relatives who argue at opposite ends of the room and stock the tables with snacks to distract them."

Omer chuckled, "You mean like a buffet of chaos? Brilliant!"

As the laughter subsided, Liana couldn't help but feel a wave of gratitude wash over her. They were more than just friends; they were a team, navigating the beautiful madness of love and weddings together.

"Okay, what about the flower arrangements?" Omer suggested, glancing at a stack of flower catalogs. "Do we want something classic, or should we go wild and throw in some neon colors?"

Joseph feigned a serious expression. "I vote for neon. Nothing says 'I love you' like a bouquet that looks like it came straight from a rave!"

Daisy shook her head, her laughter bubbling over. "Please no! I can already picture my grandmother's face if she sees a neon pink daisy. She'd think she's entered a time warp!"

"Oh, come on! We could tell her it's the latest trend in Istanbul!" Joseph shot back, and they all erupted in laughter again.

"Alright, alright," Liana said, wiping away tears of laughter. "Let's stick with something elegant but fun. Maybe soft pastels with a few unexpected pops of color—like a lovely summer garden, with just a hint of disco!"

The discussions continued, punctuated by laughter and playful banter. As they flipped through magazines and pulled up Pinterest boards, they got lost in ideas and dreams. It felt less like work and more like a celebration, each moment a reminder of how lucky they were to have one another.

"Now, the cake!" Daisy declared dramatically, waving her arms as if she were conducting an orchestra. "It has to be nothing short of a masterpiece! I demand tiers, frosting, and enough sprinkles to make a rainbow!"

Joseph nodded solemnly. "We're not just having a cake; we're having an edible work of art! Maybe we can get a sculptor to make a cake that looks like us! Just think of the Instagram likes!"
"A cake statue of ourselves?" Omer laughed. "I can already hear the comments: 'Is this the wedding or a gallery opening?'"

"Or 'They've peaked, and it's all downhill from here!'" Liana added, and they all burst into laughter again, picturing the absurdity of it all.

As the night wore on, Liana felt a deep sense of joy enveloping her. Surrounded by friends who made even the most mundane tasks feel extraordinary, she realized that the preparations were as much a part of their love story as the wedding day itself. Each planning session became a tapestry of memories, woven with threads of humor and joy, solidifying the bond they all shared.

"You know," Joseph said, leaning forward, his eyes sparkling with mischief, "we should probably have a 'Dance-Off' during the reception. It'll be like 'So You Think You Can Dance,' but with more stumbling and less talent."

Daisy burst out laughing. "I'm totally down for that! We'll have everyone show off their best moves! If nothing else, we'll get some epic blooper footage!"

"Or we could just make it a competition for the worst dancer," Liana suggested, her laughter mingling with theirs. "I volunteer myself as tribute if that's the case!"

The room was filled with their laughter and camaraderie as they dove deeper into the madness of wedding planning, unearthing the beauty of their friendship along the way. Liana looked around at her friends—at Omer, the love of her life; at Daisy, her forever cheerleader; and at Joseph, the jokester who always lightened the mood.

With each shared joke and every outrageous idea, she felt an overwhelming sense of love, not just for Omer, but for the life they were building together. The wedding would be just one day, but this journey—the laughter, the planning, the shared moments—was what truly mattered.

As the sun began to set, casting a warm golden hue across the room, Liana realized that this was it: the tapestry of their lives, vibrant with color, humor, and love. She couldn't wait to step into the future, surrounded by the people who filled her heart with joy, laughter, and endless possibilities. And with that thought, she couldn't help but feel that the best was yet to come.

Chapter 24

A Celebration of Love

"Love is a celebration of two souls finding home in each other—a quiet joy that blooms with every shared smile, every gentle touch, and every whispered promise. It is the warmth of a thousand suns, the comfort of a quiet embrace, and the unspoken vow to walk hand in hand through all the seasons of life."

The day had finally arrived, a day that had felt like a dream ever since Liana had proposed to Omer. Their wedding was set in a picturesque garden on the outskirts of Istanbul, blooming with vibrant flowers and surrounded by the soothing sounds of nature. The sun hung high in the sky, casting a golden glow over everything as if even the universe had come together to celebrate their love. It was the kind of day where the air was fragrant with roses and lavender, and everything seemed to shine a little brighter.

Liana stood in front of the mirror, taking in the reflection of her wedding dress. It was simple yet elegant, adorned with delicate lace that flowed gracefully to the ground. Her mother had once worn the same lace pattern on her wedding day, and the thought made Liana's heart swell. As she adjusted her veil, she felt a mix of emotions—excitement, nervousness, and deep, unshakable happiness. Today marked the beginning of their forever, and she wanted everything to be perfect. The way she felt for Omer was not just love; it was a sense of belonging, like she had finally found her home.

Daisy, her best friend and confidante, burst into the room, her eyes wide with admiration. *"You look stunning, Liana!"* she exclaimed, her voice cracking slightly. *"Omer won't know what hit him."* There was a teasing tone, but Liana could see the sincerity in her eyes, the way they glistened with unshed tears.

Liana laughed, a little nervously. *"I just hope I can keep it together when I see him."* She glanced at herself in the mirror again, smoothing out an invisible wrinkle on her dress. The thought of Omer waiting for her at the altar sent butterflies dancing in her stomach. Would she cry? Would he?

Daisy stepped closer, adjusting the veil over Liana's dark, wavy hair. *"You two are perfect for each other. I've never seen you this happy, Li. You deserve this."* Her tone softened, and she squeezed Liana's hand, a silent promise that she would always be there.

Liana's throat tightened with emotion. *"Thanks, Daisy,"* she whispered, her voice filled with gratitude. *"It means the world to have you by my side today. You're like my sister."*

Daisy blinked rapidly, trying not to cry. *"Stop it, or you'll make me ruin my makeup!"* She laughed, but it was clear she was holding back tears. *"Now go and make your dreams come true, alright?"*

Meanwhile, on the other side of the garden, Joseph was helping Omer prepare for the ceremony. He stood in front of Omer, adjusting his tie with a playful smirk. *"You look sharp, man. Ready to tie the knot?"* he asked, but his voice carried an underlying tone of affection.

Omer chuckled, trying to hide the mix of excitement and nerves bubbling inside him. *"I think so. I just hope I don't trip or start crying when I see her walking down the aisle,"* he admitted, half-joking, half-serious.

"You won't," Joseph reassured him, patting him on the back. *"Just focus on Liana. Remember how happy she makes you, how she looks at you like you're the only guy in the world. That's all you need to keep you steady."*

Omer smiled, a bit more at ease. *"You're right. I can't wait to see her."* And he meant it. He had pictured this moment countless times, but he still felt a rush of anticipation that made his heart race. There was something surreal about it, as if he was on the verge of stepping into a dream he never wanted to wake up from.

As the time drew closer, guests began to arrive, filling the garden with laughter and joyful chatter. There were soft murmurs of greetings, warm hugs, and delighted exclamations as friends and family reunited. The air was thick with anticipation, and Liana's heart swelled with love for all the people who had come to celebrate their union. She spotted familiar faces—friends, family, and those who had been part of their journey together. It felt like every single person present was carrying a piece of their love story, making the moment even more meaningful.

Finally, it was time. Liana took a deep breath, her heart pounding as she stepped outside. The garden looked enchanting, decorated with twinkling lights strung up between the trees and flowers in every hue imaginable. Petals were scattered across the path, a carpet of color leading to the altar where Omer stood, waiting for her. She locked eyes with him, and the rest of the world blurred into soft, dreamy edges. He looked dashing, his smile warm and eyes bright, and for a moment, she forgot to breathe.

Time seemed to stand still as she made her way toward him, her heart in sync with the soft melody that played in the background.

Joseph held her arm, walking her down the aisle, his grip tender yet firm, as if to say, *"I'm proud of you. I'm with you."*

As she approached, the world around them faded away. Omer's eyes sparkled with emotion, and Liana felt a rush of love that brought tears to her eyes. She felt the weight of every moment they had shared—every laugh, every quiet conversation, every lingering touch—and it all led to this. The realization hit her: she was marrying her best friend, the person who understood her even when she couldn't find the words.

The officiant began the ceremony, speaking about love, commitment, and the beauty of partnership. Liana's gaze never left Omer; she felt a sense of calm wash over her as they exchanged vows. *"I promise to support you, to laugh with you, and to be there for you through everything,"* she said, her voice steady, but her eyes glistening with unshed tears. *"You're my home, Omer. My greatest adventure."*

Omer's smile grew wider, his heart brimming with joy. *"And I promise to cherish you, to stand by you, and to create a life together filled with love and adventure,"* he said, his voice catching slightly. *"You've always been my light, Liana, and I can't wait to build our future together."*

As they exchanged rings, Liana felt a surge of happiness. The symbolism of their promises, the merging of their lives, was more powerful than she had ever imagined. With a soft, tender kiss, they sealed their vows, and the guests erupted in applause.

Joseph stepped forward, grinning widely. *"Ladies and gentlemen, I present to you, Mr. and Mrs. Omer!"* The cheers and laughter filled the air, echoing the joy that enveloped the couple.

The reception was a whirlwind of love and laughter. Daisy and Joseph were the perfect hosts, ensuring that everyone felt welcome and cherished. As the sun began to set, the garden transformed into a magical wonderland, with lanterns illuminating the space and a gentle breeze rustling the leaves. Tables were set under a canopy of stars, the sounds of clinking glasses and soft laughter mingling with the gentle music.

Liana and Omer shared their first dance as a married couple, swaying to a romantic melody that seemed to wrap around them like a warm embrace. They were lost in each other, surrounded by their friends and family, but in that moment, it felt as if they were the only two people in the world.

"I can't believe we're finally married," Liana whispered, her eyes sparkling with happiness. She rested her head against Omer's chest, feeling the steady rhythm of his heartbeat.

"Neither can I," Omer replied, pulling her closer as if he feared she might slip away. *"This is just the beginning, Liana. I'm so excited for*

our future. We have so many stories to write and so many places to see. As long as we're together, I know everything will be beautiful."

As the night unfolded, laughter and stories flowed freely. Joseph shared anecdotes that had everyone in stitches, recounting hilarious misadventures of Omer's youth, while Daisy captured every moment with her camera, ensuring that their memories would be preserved forever.

When it came time for the speeches, Joseph stood up, raising his glass. *"To Liana and Omer—may your love be modern enough to survive the times and old-fashioned enough to last forever!"* The room erupted in cheers, and Liana felt a rush of gratitude for the love surrounding them.

As the evening light bathed the garden in a warm glow, laughter, and chatter filled the air, creating a symphony of joy that perfectly matched the atmosphere of love. Friends and family gathered around the newlyweds, their smiles wide and hearts full. Liana and Omer stood hand in hand, their eyes sparkling with happiness as they basked in the moment.

Joseph and Daisy, ever the lively duo, stood a little to the side, animatedly discussing their plans for a surprise performance. "We need to make this unforgettable," Joseph declared, a mischievous glint in his eyes. Daisy clapped her hands excitedly. "I know just the song! Let's do it!"

With a swift exchange of glances, the two friends made their way to the center of the gathering, where a makeshift stage had been set up. The guests, sensing something special was about to happen, hushed their conversations and turned their attention toward the pair.

"Ladies and gentlemen!" Joseph called out, his voice booming with enthusiasm. "We have a little something for our beloved Liana and Omer!"

Daisy chimed in, her smile infectious. "It's a celebration of love, and we want to share it with you all!"

With that, they launched into a heartfelt song they had crafted just for the occasion, capturing the essence of Liana and Omer's love story.

(Verse 1: Joseph)
In this dance of love, where two hearts entwine,
We gather here today, to witness the divine.
With laughter and with joy, let the music play,
For Liana and Omer, this is their day.

(Chorus: Daisy & Joseph)
So raise your voices high, let the world hear,
A celebration of love, filled with cheer.
With every step you take, know you're never alone,
In this beautiful journey, you've found your home.

(Verse 2: Daisy)
From the bustling streets of Istanbul to this moment so bright,
Your love has blossomed into a radiant light.
Through every challenge faced, you've found your way,
Hand in hand together, come what may.

(Chorus: Daisy & Joseph)
So raise your voices high, let the world hear,
A celebration of love, filled with cheer.
With every step you take, know you're never alone,
In this beautiful journey, you've found your home.

(Bridge: Joseph)
Now here's to the memories, the laughter, and the tears,
To the moments that brought you together through the years.
May your love keep growing, like a river that flows,
In this garden of dreams, let your happiness grow.

(Final Chorus: Daisy & Joseph)
So raise your voices high, let the world hear,
A celebration of love, filled with cheer.
With every step you take, know you're never alone,
In this beautiful journey, you've found your home.

As they finished the last note, the crowd erupted into applause, cheers ringing out as Liana and Omer exchanged glances, their eyes glistening with emotion. The performance encapsulated their journey beautifully, making their hearts swell with love.

Daisy and Joseph bowed theatrically, and Liana rushed forward, enveloping them both in a tight embrace. "You two are incredible!" she exclaimed, laughter bubbling from her lips. "Thank you for making this day even more special!"

Omer joined in, grinning widely. "You brought the house down. We couldn't have asked for a better surprise."

As the evening continued, the garden filled with joy and laughter, the essence of love flowing freely in the air. It was a perfect moment, one that would be etched in their hearts forever, as they celebrated the beginning of their beautiful journey together.

Later, as they stepped away from the festivities for a moment of quiet, Liana leaned her head against Omer's shoulder, a content smile on her face. *"I couldn't have imagined a more perfect day,"* she murmured, watching the lanterns sway gently in the breeze, their light flickering like fireflies.

Omer kissed the top of her head, his lips lingering. *"Neither could I. Thank you for making me the happiest man alive. I don't know what I did to deserve you, but I promise to spend the rest of my life showing you just how much you mean to me."*

As the stars twinkled above them, Liana knew they had created a beautiful beginning. Surrounded by love, friendship, and the promise of a lifetime together, she felt an overwhelming sense of joy. The journey ahead would undoubtedly have its challenges, but she was ready to face them all—together with Omer, hand in hand, heart in heart. In that moment, she understood that love wasn't just about finding someone to share your life with; it was about building a life together, brick by brick, moment by moment. And as she stood there with Omer, under a sky full of stars, she knew they were ready for everything the future would bring.

It was a day they would remember for the rest of their lives—not just because it was their wedding, but because it was the day their love story truly began, surrounded by everyone who had been a part of their journey, by every small kindness, every shared laugh, and every wordless moment that had brought them to this point.

Hand in hand, they walked back towards the celebration, ready to begin their forever.

Epilogue

A Tapestry of Love

As Liana and Omer navigated through the bustling Istanbul airport, the excitement of their wedding still radiated from them like a warm glow. Liana turned to Omer, her eyes sparkling with mischief. "Do you think anyone will believe we just got married? We could totally pull off the whole 'newlywed glow' thing."

Omer chuckled, his hand instinctively finding hers. "Only if you stop calling me 'Omer' and start referring to me as 'Your Husband.'"

She laughed, playfully nudging him. "I might just start doing that. Your Husband, can you please grab our bags?"

"Your Husband is on it!" he replied with mock seriousness, darting off to retrieve their luggage.

As they stood waiting for their bags, Liana looked around at the throng of travelers, a mix of excitement and exhaustion etched on their faces. "It feels surreal, doesn't it?" she said, leaning against Omer, who wrapped an arm around her shoulders.

"Yeah," he agreed, his voice softening. "One moment, we were surrounded by our friends and family, exchanging vows under the Istanbul sky, and now we're back to reality. But I wouldn't trade any of it for the world."

The carousel started to spin, and their bags appeared, bringing with them a sense of normalcy. As they collected their belongings, Joseph and Daisy approached, their faces lighting up with enthusiasm.

"Did you two just get back from a honeymoon or what?" Daisy teased, her eyes glimmering.

"More like a whirlwind of love and a little too much baklava," Omer grinned, pulling Liana closer.

Joseph held out a small bouquet of flowers. "Welcome back! We couldn't let you arrive without a little something to remind you of your fabulous wedding."

Liana accepted the bouquet, her heart swelling with gratitude. "You guys are the best! Thank you for everything."

As they made their way out of the airport, Liana felt the weight of the world lifting off her shoulders. The anticipation of returning home together buzzed in the air. The city that awaited them felt different now, filled with possibilities and the promise of a life shared—no longer just dreams, but a beautiful reality they had crafted together.

Liana stood on the balcony of their New York apartment, she looked out over the city that had witnessed so many chapters of her life. The evening sky was a breathtaking palette of oranges and purples, fading into deep indigo as the stars began to twinkle. It was a moment of stillness, a quiet reflection after the whirlwind of emotions and experiences that had defined her journey.

Their time in Istanbul felt like a dream—a vivid tapestry woven from threads of love, adventure, and profound connections. Every corner of that vibrant city held a memory, a lesson, a piece of their shared story. From the bustling streets filled with the aroma of spices to the serene beauty of the Bosphorus at sunset, Istanbul embraced them, nurturing their love as it blossomed.

She thought back to their wedding day—the way Omer had looked at her as she walked down the aisle, the tears of joy in his eyes, and the vows they had exchanged, promising to support and uplift each other through every twist and turn life would present.

At that moment, standing before their friends and family, Liana felt an overwhelming sense of belonging, as if the universe had conspired to bring them together at that precise moment in time.

But it wasn't just the wedding that marked a turning point; it was the journey they had taken to get there. Liana recalled their late-night conversations filled with dreams and fears, the moments of vulnerability when they shared their innermost thoughts, each revelation strengthening the bond that tied them together. Istanbul had been more than just a backdrop; it was a crucible that had forged their love, pushing them to confront their deepest insecurities and embrace the beauty of their imperfections. Throughout this journey, it was Rumi's words that echoed in their hearts, guiding them. They had found solace in his poetry, a gentle reminder that love was both a profound mystery and a simple truth. His words had taught them that to love deeply was to embrace the unknown, to find joy in the unexpected, and to seek connection beyond the surface.

Returning to New York was both comforting and exhilarating. The familiar sights felt renewed in their significance. This city had been the backdrop of their individual stories, but now it was the canvas upon which they would paint their future together. Liana's heart raced with anticipation of what lay ahead, a new chapter waiting to be written.

One evening, they found themselves at the very café where they had spent countless hours talking and dreaming. It was a space filled with laughter and warmth, the perfect setting to commemorate their journey. Over cups of rich coffee, they shared stories about their favorite moments in Istanbul—the sun-drenched afternoons spent exploring the Grand Bazaar, the late nights wandering through the winding streets of Sultanahmet, and the breathtaking view from the Galata Tower that had left them both speechless.

Omer reached across the table, his hand enveloping hers. "Do *you remember that day we got lost in the bazaar?*" he asked, a mischievous grin spreading across his face.

Liana laughed, the sound bright and full of life. "*How could I forget? You tried to haggle for that ridiculous lamp, and I thought we might never find our way back!*"

"*But we did, didn't we?*" he said, his gaze locking onto hers. "*And we discovered so much along the way. Isn't that what life is about?*"

At that moment, Liana realized that their love was much like that journey through the bazaar—sometimes chaotic and unpredictable, yet filled with wonder and beauty. They had navigated the twists and turns, discovering hidden treasures in the form of shared laughter and silent understanding. It was as Rumi had said, "*Where there is ruin, there is hope for a treasure.*" They had found that treasure in each other, in their ability to turn every obstacle into an opportunity for growth.

As they spoke, Liana felt an overwhelming wave of gratitude wash over her. She thought of Joseph and Daisy, who had stood by them through every challenge and celebration. Their friendships had anchored her, providing strength when she felt unsure and encouragement when she doubted herself. Each person they had met along the way, each story shared during their *"Whispers of the Heart"* gatherings, had contributed to a rich tapestry of connection that now felt integral to their lives.

"What do you think our next adventure will be?" Liana asked, her eyes sparkling with excitement.

Omer smiled, a twinkle in his eye. "I *don't know, but I do know this: wherever we go, we'll go together.*"

The words resonated deep within her, echoing the promise they had made on their wedding day. They were partners in every sense—navigating the unknown, celebrating each triumph, and supporting one another through challenges.

As the weeks turned into months, they continued to explore their city with the same curiosity they had brought to Istanbul. Each weekend became an opportunity for new adventures—discovering hidden gems in neighborhoods they had never explored, attending local art shows, and supporting community events. With every shared experience, they cultivated a deeper understanding of themselves and each other, growing stronger as a couple.

One crisp autumn afternoon, Liana found herself wandering through Central Park, the leaves a vibrant mosaic of colors. She paused to take in the beauty around her, the laughter of children playing, and couples walking hand in hand, all wrapped in the warmth of the season.

"Can you believe we're living our dream?" she thought aloud, capturing the moment in her heart.

Omer joined her, wrapping his arms around her waist. "I *can because we've built this together. Each step, each decision, has brought us closer to this reality.*"

Liana smiled, resting her head against his shoulder. In that serene moment, she felt a sense of fulfillment that transcended words. Life was not just about the milestones; it was about the journey itself—the quiet moments of connection, the shared laughter, and the love that wrapped around them like a warm *embrace. She remembered a line from Rumi that had once been just words on a page: "Lovers don't finally meet somewhere. They're in each other all along."* It had taken time, but she understood it now. Their journey wasn't about arriving; it was about unfolding, revealing the layers of their love.

With each passing day, she felt the wounds of the past begin to heal, replaced by a profound sense of hope and possibility. They had faced their fears, confronted their insecurities, and emerged stronger together. Liana understood now that love was not merely a feeling; it was a choice they made every day—to support, uplift, and cherish one another in all their imperfections.

As the city buzzed around them, she thought back to Rumi's words, words she had initially turned to for solace. While they had guided her, she now understood that her journey was uniquely her own. It was a story woven with love, resilience, and a deep connection to the world around her.

Standing there with Omer, she realized that life was a beautiful tapestry, each thread representing a moment of joy, a lesson learned, or a connection forged. Together, they were crafting a masterpiece, a story that would continue to unfold, rich with adventures yet to come. It was as if Rumi's wisdom had been a map, leading them to this point, but now they were writing their verses, painting their pictures, and dancing to a rhythm only they could hear.

As the sun began to set, casting a golden hue over the park, Liana squeezed Omer's hand, a silent promise that they would navigate this journey together. No matter where the winds of life took them, they would face it as partners, united in love.

In the heart of New York, amidst the chaos and beauty, they had found their home—not just in the city, but in each other. And with that realization, Liana smiled, her heart full, knowing that the best was yet to come.

As the last rays of the sun dipped below the horizon, casting a soft, warm glow over the city, Liana closed her eyes and breathed in the crisp autumn air. She felt Omer's steady heartbeat against her, a rhythm that had become her sanctuary. In that moment, she understood that their love was not just a series of fleeting moments but an endless journey, one that would grow and evolve, transcending time and place. They had been two wandering souls who found solace in each other's embrace, and now, together, they were writing a love story that would endure— one that would be whispered in quiet corners, celebrated in bursts of laughter, and cherished in the gentle, knowing smiles they would share for years to come. And as the city lights began to shimmer, illuminating the path ahead, Liana knew that wherever life led them, they would always find their way back to this—their own quiet.

Liana opened her diary, a warm smile brightening her face as she began to write:

A Tapestry of Us

Love, a gentle whisper in the storm,
A warm embrace when the world grows cold,
It blooms in the cracks where light is reborn,
A quiet promise, steadfast and bold.

Faith, the unseen thread that binds,
Woven through the tapestry of days,
It carries us through darkened times,
A guiding star in the winding maze.

Solace, found in a familiar gaze,
In laughter shared and hands entwined,
A refuge through life's winding ways,
Where hearts find rest, and souls align.

Peace, the stillness between each breath,
A lullaby sung by the moonlit sea,
It fills the spaces that linger beneath,
A gentle sigh, serene and free.

Together they dance, entwined and true,
Love, faith, solace, peace—they bloom anew,
For in the journey, their souls find grace,
A home in each other, a sacred place.

Through Istanbul's streets to New York's light,
They walk hand in hand, day and night,
Crafting a story, pure and divine,
A love that transcends both space and time.

THE END

"And in the end, it wasn't the answers we found that mattered, but the questions we dared to ask with open hearts."

www.ingramcontent.com/pod-product-compliance
Lightning Source LLC
Chambersburg PA
CBHW071409300726
48976CB00006B/2038